SCORCHING THE EARTH

KTS #4

ELISE FABER

SCORCHING THE EARTH
BY ELISE FABER
Newsletter sign-up

SCORCHING THE EARTH
Copyright © 2021 Elise Faber
Print ISBN-13: 978-1-63749-038-9
Ebook ISBN-13: 978-1-63749-037-2
Cover Art by Jena Brignola

KTS SERIES

Riding The Edge
Crossing The Line
Leveling The Field
Scorching The Earth

CHAPTER ONE

Time: 0348hrs
Location: Fuck if she knew
Situation: FUBAR

LILY

THE DIGITAL CLOCK on the wall was really not helpful.

I didn't need to know what time they were dragging a knife over my skin, digging the tip in a way that was designed to draw out the pain.

The hand clenching that knife passed in front of my face, a tattoo inked on the space between thumb and forefinger, a flash of black ink—a crescent moon, a set of scales, a line written in Latin.

One I was intimately familiar with because I'd spent months researching anything to do with this group whose sole purpose seemed to be destroying everything I had been working for. Destroying the organization I was a part of, eliminating and

CHAPTER TWO

Lily, Three Weeks Before

"WHAT ARE YOU DOING?"

I glanced up at the open door to my office and knew my expression was guilty, but it was just so sweet!

"Nothing," I said quickly, wiping my eye and affecting casualness as Hannah moved toward me.

Slyly, I minimized the window where I'd been—admittedly —spying on my teammates Leo and Jesse, who'd fought their attraction, had overcome some serious obstacles, and finally —*finally*, the stubborn fools!—found their happy together.

They were just…so sweet.

Leo was so sweet.

Jesse was sweet.

But mostly…Leo was taking sweet to the next level.

How did I know this?

Because I'd helped him with the surprise, helped him pick out a dress and shoes, one that would melt soft-at-heart Jesse's…well, *heart*. And Hannah, my team leader and beautiful blonde who screamed that she could kick some serious ass with just a—and it must be said *silent*—glance was walking across my office, thunderclouds in her hazel eyes. But even my BAMF of a boss and friend had assisted in the romance as well, filling Jesse's room with flameless candles and flowers.

Not to mention locking Leo and Jesse in a room together when they'd been too stubborn to see they were perfect for each other.

Leo, of course, was mostly responsible for the current romantic situation. He'd had the idea to surprise his woman, and he'd picked out a necklace (though he'd let me peek into the box). I wasn't sure what the deal with owls was, but considering Jesse hadn't stopped touching it the entire time I'd spied on them through the cameras that lined the walls of the compound as they'd walked hand in hand across the courtyard, I knew she was happy with it.

But I digressed.

Because Hannah rested a hip on my desk, her eyes flicking to my screen.

Ha.

I was ahead of her.

Because there was nothing to see there.

Thank God for quick trigger fingers and…I mentally wrinkled my nose because there were *so* many innuendos my teammates could make about that particular expression and so much shit that would be given lest I say it aloud. Mostly because yeah, I was a lesbian, yeah, I was good with my fingers and… yeah, I gave my teammates plenty of teasing about their various extremities, love interests, and sexual prowess (Prowesses? Prowesi?). Anywho, the point was that I probably deserved any trigger-finger-teasing.

But Hannah, my team leader, the woman I had been crushing on hard—for fucking *years*—was my team leader because she was smart as hell.

Beautiful.

Strong.

Capable.

Tortured.

My kryptonite.

So much that from the moment I'd met her, I'd wanted to wave my hand fiercely through the air and declare, "I volunteer for tribute! I have *all* the love to give. Let me take care of those darkened shadows in your beautiful hazel eyes!"

Her eyes flicked from the screen back to mine, something I couldn't read in her expression. Something that turned out to be sneaky...and smart, dammit. Because she asked, "You want to get some food?" and when I nodded and stood up, she reached for the mouse and opened the window I'd minimized.

Which was, of course, still on the camera feed of Leo and Jesse.

They'd been standing close together when I'd clicked away before, Jesse crying after what had probably been sweet words from Leo (damn cameras without audio, otherwise I could have listened in. Also, note to self, convince the bigwigs to invest in cameras with audio). Now, however, they were dancing under the moonlight, their arms wrapped tightly around each other.

I sighed happily.

Seriously. So. Freaking. Sweet.

Hannah, seemingly unaffected by all that sweet, glared down at me. "You're impossible."

"Because I have a heart and love a romantic ending?" I asked lightly.

Because I had a heart that she owned, even if she didn't know it, and was desperate—*desperate!*—for a romantic ending.

With Hannah.

It didn't have to be anything grand, anything so dramatic as a dress and dancing under the moonlight. I'd take bingeing movies in bed, cuddled up together, bellies full of too much popcorn. I'd take cooking a meal together, rolling our eyes over an inside joke.

I'd take...her mouth across mine.

Gentle. Intense. A brush. Her tongue tangling with mine. And anything in between.

I just wanted Hannah.

Who was sighing and rolling those gorgeous hazel eyes of hers, her blond ponytail fluttering behind her when she shook her head. "Come on, sap," she said, clicking to close the camera feed rather than just minimizing it. "Let's eat."

I stuck out my bottom lip. "I don't want to."

Hannah sighed. "What *do* you want?"

You.

I was desperate to say it, but I knew it wouldn't make the least bit of difference. Hannah didn't do relationships, and she certainly didn't do relationships with subordinates.

But circling back to that volunteering for tribute...oh, and the fact that I'd been in love with her from the moment I'd laid eyes on her.

See? I *was* a hopeless romantic.

Maybe hopeless was the keyword in that statement.

I'd walked into KTS six years before, ready for my training, and had seen her knocking a man nearly twice her size to the mats in the gym. She hadn't struggled or so much as took an extra breath, hadn't ended up with even a hair out of place.

I'd arrested, felt my heart roll over and expose its vulnerable underbelly.

Then she'd smiled, winked at me.

And I'd fallen deep.

She was intelligent, gorgeous, funny, a total badass who still managed to be kind and empathetic...and also closed down to anything that resembled love. At least overtly, because I knew she loved our entire team. She would die to ensure that we would live and do it in a heartbeat.

So, the love was there. Her past hadn't killed off her love for friends.

She might not be overt about it; she might not emote like me. It might be buried, but it was wholly present.

She'd overcome her tortured past to love us.

As teammates.

Because romantic love? *That* wasn't present or buried under several layers of concrete. I was starting to think it wasn't there at all, that it would *never* be there, despite that being the love I was desperate for.

The love I craved. The love I was beginning to accept wasn't ever going to happen. Not for me. Not between Hannah *and* me.

Which made me feel super-duper awesome. Go me! Get all mopey and depressed just because I wanted something someone wasn't capable of giving. Something that wasn't my place to demand because it needed to be freely given.

Yeah, I'd yearned.

But I wasn't Hannah, hadn't lived her life.

So, I didn't get a say. Not. One.

Grimacing, I grabbed my cell and started for the door.

Hannah sighed again. "What is it?"

I frowned, glanced back over my shoulder. "What's what?"

"Why are you doing Sad Face?"

Damn. I should have made certain to do that grimace internally.

Because I couldn't tell her I was in love with her and wanted to ban all those shadows darkening her soul, to wrap her up in so much love that she would fall for me back, so I just said, "Of course I'm doing Sad Face. You interrupted my quota of romance for the day." I chuckled.

It sounded fake.

Crap.

Hannah strolled over to me, not stopping until she was close enough for me to see the faint scar just above her cheekbone. I knew it was from a flying piece of shrapnel on a mission the previous year. A mission that had bought me eighteen stitches. A mission where she'd refused to get her cut looked at before I was treated and cleared. A cut that turned into a scar because she'd cared about me before herself.

See?

She had love to give.

And that was why it was so fucking hard to let go of my fantasy.

That fantasy being that she'd turn to me one day, declare her undying love, and then we'd be dancing under the moonlight, our happy ending beginning.

Fingers on my jaw, turning my face toward hers. "Tell me the truth, Lil."

If only.

That would buy her a whole truck of concrete to reinforce the walls around her heart...and probably me a transfer to another team.

I shrugged. "I'm hungry is all."

She narrowed her eyes.

I started to turn away, to hit that exit and regroup, and—

Then I was pinned to the wall, her hands on my shoulders, her body almost flush to mine. My heart skipped and began pounding rapidly. The backs of my knees went sweaty. The hair on my arms lifted.

"Tell me," she demanded.

And it *was* a demand.

One that had heat coiling through me, starting from my fingertips that ached to stroke over her skin, traveling up my arms, dancing across my cheeks, my lips, my throat. Moving down, drifting over my breasts, scorching through my center, and finally, coming to a halt just between my thighs.

Need and heat...and so much unrequited love.

I was pathetic.

This was pathetic.

But when I went to move away, her hazel eyes darkened, going more chocolate than the usual green. "Tell me," she said, softer now, her head dipping down. I smelled mint on her breath, knew she'd been chewing a piece of her favorite spearmint gum. Not peppermint or wintergreen or cool mint swirl.

Spearmint.

That was all that she wanted.

"Lil," she murmured.

I melted, especially when her body moved closer, when she pressed her lithe, strong curves into mine, making my pussy clench and my skin tighten until it felt three sizes too small. "It's nothing," I managed to croak out.

"*Lily*," she warned, fingers gripping my shoulders a little tighter.

I lifted my chin, began to repeat the lie. "It's—"

Another squeeze. "Don't bullshit me, baby."

This time heat dumped over my head by the bucketful, dousing my hair and then sliding like honey over my skin, dripping down my thighs, my shins, all the way to my toes. Baby. She'd called me *baby*. I sucked in a breath. "We should go."

Hannah stepped closer, pinned me more firmly, one of her hands sliding up to cup the side of my neck. "We're not going anywhere until you tell me why you're sad."

My throat went tighter, heart thudding against my ribs.

"*Lily*." A warning.

An order.

And paired with her so close, her body to mine, her hands on me, I answered. I *had* to, though it could be said that my words were more rasp than reply, belying everything she was doing to me, to my body, to my heart. "I think you know," I whispered.

She growled, those fingers tightening on the side of my neck, nails lightly scouring over my skin. "Tell. Me."

And...the truth flew out, just slid right off my tongue.

"I'm in love with you," I whispered.

Her eyes went wide. Her mouth fell open.

But she didn't move, didn't say a word. At least not until I found myself lifting a hand, tracing my thumb lightly over that scar on her cheek.

As though I could heal the old wound.

Heal *all* her old wounds.

Please.

God.

Let me.

She shuddered, her breath hot and damp on my lips . . . and then her mouth found mine.

CHAPTER THREE

LILY

NO SOONER HAD Hannah's lips touched mine, her tongue sliding into my mouth, her hand drifting up my side, fingers teasing the outside of my breast...then she was pulling away.

Chest heaving—hers, *mine.*

Warmth in those hazel eyes.

No.

Not warmth.

Fury.

She took a step back. Another.

Held my gaze as she deliberately wiped the back of her hand across her mouth.

Stab.

I felt the knife enter my heart, just as if she'd thrust it home in real life.

And after that blow was delivered...

She spun on her heel and strode through my office door.

———

I CAUGHT a glimpse of a fancy dress.

I heard the giggle.

The soft *smack* of a kiss.

Leo's husky whisper.

Love.

True love.

And great, now I sounded like the officiant from *The Princess Bride*.

Wuv. Twue wuv will follow you forevah.

I clutched my slice of medicinal chocolate cake (medicinal to me, okay?) to my chest—or my plate, rather—and tucked myself deeper into the shadows.

Was it my third piece of medicinal chocolate cake?

Yes.

Did I make myself walk to the mess each time I got another slice because I liked to pretend that I was being healthy and burning off calories by making that trek?

Also, yes.

Was my ass getting bigger from all that self-medicating with chocolate?

Anyone want to guess?

Jesse giggled again, and I held back my jealousy by pure dint. They deserved it. Just because I was a giant mopey pants who'd declared my love and then made the object of that love wipe off our first kiss with purposeful disgust didn't mean I needed to be a jerk about it.

I *needed* to be happy for them.

For the rest of my teammates who were all so lovingly matched.

Not only for my fluffy unicorn-loving, romance-craving soul, but for me. Because I was a good person who'd been taught to look out for other people, to care about them, and just because I hadn't found a person who'd do that for me—

The door slammed.

And luckily, I didn't have to go further down that train of thought.

Instead, I slipped out of the shadows, clutched my plate of chocolate cake like the national treasure it was, and moved to my room.

Thinking that I was so happy for Jess and Leo.

Knowing they both deserved the love they'd found in each other.

Knowing that the type of love, of happiness, of intense, soul-linking connection my friends had found probably wasn't in the cards for me.

Because...I didn't inspire that type of emotion.

That wasn't me trying to be dramatic or feeling woe is me (remember, I'd already self-medicated copiously with chocolate, the woes had passed).

I just...was *me*.

Me was enough. Hell, *me* was pretty fucking great. Confidence wasn't my issue. I was pretty, smart, could hit a target from two hundred yards away even with a changeable wind. I knew a plethora of pressure points...and could hold my own in hand-to-hand combat against multiple attackers—and not just because I'd practiced with teammates on base.

I'd fought. I'd kicked ass.

I was a badass.

Not as much as Hannah, of course, but I was good at what I did. And I was a good person. *And* if I could spend a moment being superficial, I filled out my sports bra and my jeans in a way that meant I was feminine and curvy, even despite the fact that I worked out a lot and was strong, and—

I was the shit.

Seriously, *the shit*.

I just didn't...inspire grand gestures or big feelings.

Yeah, people liked me. Yeah, I got along with everyone. I inspired friendship, not devotion.

I just...

Right.

That was a lot of *I justs*. Too many *I justs* for my own peace of mind.

I slapped my hand on the lock outside my door, pushed inside, and proceeded to down my final piece of cake.

And because I was trying to ignore those *I justs* and the way they made me feel, I pulled out my Kindle.

And I read.

And I lost myself in a world that was fictional and safe and where happy endings were guaranteed.

And all the while I tried to pretend I wasn't gutted inside.

———

I WOKE KNOWING the next day was going to be brutal.

I wasn't prepared for the full ice storm that was Hannah.

Silent treatment would have been better.

Instead, I received frigid politeness instead of anything approaching a normal interaction. No morning coffee and going over my research. No meeting me and jumping on the treadmill next to mine when I hit the gym before lunch. No dragging me out of my office when I worked too late and making sure I ate dinner.

Just steady eye contact during the team meeting finalizing the last-minute details before we flew out late that evening to continue our research into the Moldovan Five—the group of agents we suspected were the key to all the betrayals on missions and the infiltration of our organization, KTS. The agents who we suspected were behind or were involved with the group who made their money via human trafficking and drug rings.

Awesome former colleagues, huh?

But we'd cracked this lead. We'd crack them too, get the information out of them, and shut down the ring, ferret out any other traitors at KTS.

And then we'd get back to saving the world.

Just like that.

The thought had made me smile during the meeting—which had earned me a wicked scowl courtesy of Hannah, who had made it clear she was strictly business in all communications.

The kiss hadn't happened.

She would make certain to erase it from history.

Concrete walls had slammed down behind a pretty hazel gaze, that truckload of cement I'd been joking about earlier exchanged for a trainload, or maybe a barge load. Either way, she'd been cold, those eyes frosted, her normally lush lips pressed flat. Absolutely no amusement dancing across her face. We didn't exchange secret looks to express a shared inside joke, and I respected the concrete, the barbed wires and spikes. I didn't smile or snort when someone said something that could go straight innuendo. I didn't give shit.

She gave me strictly business, and I gave it right back.

To the rest of the world, we would have seemed completely normal.

Hannah, certainly, because I supposed, without the shit-giving and snark, I might have come off a bit subdued.

But my teammates were in enough of a love haze that they didn't pick up on either of us being off.

Me? Oh, I read what she was projecting loud and clear.

I knew it was a message.

The kiss was a mistake.

One that wouldn't be repeated.

Something she'd said—straight out in those exact words after the meeting wrapped. Literally, pulling me aside, her fingers gripping my arm and pressing me to the wall in a way that had made my heart skip a beat (because stupid romantic soul, stupid heart that wouldn't be denied) at least until I saw the deadly icicles in her gaze. They were perched on the roof of the isolated cavern of her eyes, ready to break free, sail down through the air, and impale me if I made one wrong move.

I knew then that Hannah would transfer me to a new team without a second thought.

Regardless of our history, our friendship, our years as teammates, mine as her second-in-command. Regardless of the mission currently in play.

She would cut me loose. Easily. Quickly. Without remorse.

All because I'd stepped over her careful barrier.

Even without her saying any of that out loud, I knew. I didn't need her fingers digging into my upper arm, her icy eyes, nor her hard tone when she said, "You and me. *Never* again."

My lips had parted to tell her I got that.

She shook me before I managed to respond. "And get the other thing out of your head."

The *other thing* being that I loved her.

Right.

If only it were that easy.

Still, I'd nodded, waited until those cold eyes released me… and then I'd gone back to my office to continue researching before our flight out that evening, only stepping out thirty minutes before our go time to pack a bag.

Thirty minutes because I only needed fifteen.

I'd packed more times in my life than I could count.

And anyway, my go bag was basically always ready. I only had to throw in a few chargers, a backup battery, my toothpaste, and face wash.

The rest of that thirty minutes was spent checking and double-checking my weapons in the locker room.

One that wasn't—unfortunately for me—empty.

Hannah stood in her stall, duffle on the bench, backpack at her feet when I entered. Jesse and Leo, Linc and Olive, Ava and Dan, Laila and Ryker would be in soon. I knew that. It didn't make this any more comfortable.

But I was a badass secret agent.

I smiled in the face of discomfort and…well, *smiled.*

"I wrote a song about a tortilla," I said—to my locker, but I still said *something* to break the taut silence.

Silence that didn't stay broken after I dropped that lead-in.

I checked the ammo in my spare magazines, clipped two to my thighs, tucked the rest of them into my pack. "Actually," I finished the punchline quietly, "it's more of a *wrap*."

My gaze flicked up from where it had been carefully contemplating the zipper of my backpack, saw that Hannah was doing her own study of canvas and metal and plastic.

And. I. Kept. Going.

"Why can't a nose be twelve inches long?" I asked.

Her eyes slid to mine for one brief moment.

Then she spun, faced her locker.

"Because then it'd be *a foot*."

I forced a chuckle.

One, because it wasn't funny. Two, because...*kill me now*. Three, because—

I didn't get to three, thankfully.

The door to the locker room was pulled open, and Ava walked through, her sniper rifle casually tossed over one shoulder, as though she were carrying a purse. Dan was on her heels, and I didn't miss the hickey on his jaw.

Nor did I miss the satisfied gleam in Leo's eyes when he walked through the door holding hands with Jesse.

And Olive's cheeks flushed pink, Linc trailing with a self-satisfied expression.

And Laila's ponytail slightly askew, Ryker following her, his shirt buttoned up all wrong.

Fuck, if happy endings hadn't thrown up all over this base.

Fuck, if I didn't wish I was right in the middle of one.

"Dominic good?" I asked, forcing that longing down as I asked Olive about the teenager who had recently become her ward. Dominic had saved Olive on one of the missions that had gone bad because of a now-deceased and traitorous agent, Daniel.

That pink faded from her cheeks, and Olive smiled at me. "All good. Tom's"—one of the older agents who lived and worked strictly on base—"taken Dom under his wing. He'll be good till we get back."

I nodded, glad for that, glad for Tom. He was a good guy and an important part of why we were inching forward to solving this shit.

Not to mention, Dom was a good kid whose life had taken a shit turn because of Daniel. He deserved to have safety and some stability and people looking after him.

"I'm—" I began.

"Time to go," Hannah cut in, shouldering her pack and grabbing her duffle. Without a look back, she turned for the doors that led to the garage and pushed through.

"Apparently, Hannah's ready," Leo said dryly.

We all chuckled because it was true, because that part of Hannah's behavior wasn't out of the ordinary. When she was ready, we'd all better be, too. When she was done, she was done. When it was time to focus on work, we all got on the same page and focused on work.

Which was why, aside from the quip and the short burst of chuckles, we all hauled ass and got our shit packed, headed into the garage, and loaded into the SUVs.

And, because this was my life (at the moment, a special brand of hell), Laila, Ryker, and her team loaded into their SUV. My team loaded into another, Hannah into the driver's seat, as usual. Jesse and Leo slid into the middle seat. Linc hopped into the back with Olive (because even though she was technically on Laila's team, he and Olive were in *love* and joined at the hip...especially on joint missions like this...to the private KTS airport—where she would join her team as they flew out to San Francisco for their portion of the assignment while we headed for Ukraine).

Which left...the front passenger spot for me.

Joy.

CHAPTER FOUR

Hannah

THAT WOULD MAKE IT A WRAP.

The woman was a total dork.

I liked her.

Too much.

But she was brightness, and I was dark.

She cracked jokes. I silenced a locker room and was a control freak when it came down to everything in my life.

And her lips tasted like cotton candy.

Cotton *fucking* candy.

What the hell did I do with that?

Or the fact that the glide of her tongue against mine had me wetter than I'd ever been, my nipples tingling, my fingers aching to stroke her naked skin.

So strong.

That urge had been so fucking strong that I'd known I couldn't allow myself that.

I couldn't allow myself that taste, that touch, that glimpse into what might be.

Because we never *could* be.

Because then it would be a foot.

God. Lily was such a fucking dork. And beautiful on the inside and out, a smart and fully capable woman. My equal in so many ways.

Except that she was good, and I was bad.

And I needed to stop thinking about Lily.

I needed to focus on the mission, on tracking down the Moldovan Five, on making certain the moles and traitors inside KTS were tracked down.

I needed to focus on making the world safe.

For Lily.

———

THE PLANE ZIPPED across the Atlantic, heading to Eastern Europe where it would touch down in a nondescript airport near another KTS base, this one in Ukraine.

We would bring in our agent—Ken Rochester—haul his ass to base, and hopefully find out what his link to Daniel had been, and what his connection was to the attacks on KTS, to the drug smuggling and human trafficking.

Then we would question the rest of those fuckers—though they would be in bases around the world, interrogated by Laila's team, by Jeff's and Skye's teams (two agents Laila and I trusted with our lives...and with their help, we would hopefully find the key to this fucked up situation). Laila's team was in San Francisco. Jeff's in Puerto Rico. Skye's in South Africa.

Daniel, the traitor who'd ended up dead a few months ago, had been on a mission with those four other men.

A mission after which all four of those men had "retired" or gone MIA.

Four men our team had tracked down—Jesse, mainly, who'd become an absolute dog to a bone in locating them.

Four men who, hopefully, had the answers.

Who *would* have the answers.

Because I was fucking tired of having the people I worked with in danger. I was tired of having the people I cared about come back from missions injured or traumatized. I was tired of taking time away from trying to keep the world safe in order to ferret out rot from an organization I'd devoted my life to.

And more importantly, I was tired of good men and women dying.

A fucking group of bad guys who were preventing us from doing our jobs.

I didn't join KTS to chase shadows, to constantly be looking over my shoulder, wondering and worried that the traitors would be a step ahead of us.

I joined the organization to make a difference, to help people because I was in a position where I could.

Not to look amongst our own ranks, searching for traitors.

Movement in the aisle.

I slit my eyes, watched Lily walk to the back of the plane.

It was quiet, almost everyone sleeping—or in Leo's case, watching some movie, his headphones in. Everyone, of course, being Linc and Jesse and the one flight attendant.

Hopefully, the pilots weren't out.

So *everyone* was three.

And yeah, that wasn't a precise description, but I wasn't really thinking about precise.

Because every cell in my body was currently engaged in a tug of war.

To keep my ass in the seat.

To stand up and follow Lily down the aisle.

And then it wasn't a tug of war so much as it was one end letting loose, the other team falling backward into a giant puddle of mud.

The end that let go?

It wasn't the smart end, the prudent end.

Because then I was standing and following Lily down the aisle.

I followed her on silent feet, my movements hidden not only because of my training, but because of the plane's engines.

And probably because Lily trusted everyone on board implicitly.

She didn't need to be on high alert.

Lily slipped into the small bedroom at the back of the plane. This had been modified into a command center for the team, monitors and computers bolted onto a table. The seats out front could lie flat, which meant it was easy for the team to catch some shut-eye, especially when we'd all been trained to grab sleep when and where we could. But back here, it was all business.

I slid through into the room behind her, caught the door, and leaned back against the frame. I watched her sit down in one of the chairs, plug in her laptop to one of the monitors, and start working.

She'd been pulling a lot of hours lately.

We all had.

But Lily, in particular, I'd had to pull away from her research more than a handful of times over the last weeks and months. Mostly when I couldn't take how dark the circles under her eyes became. So, I'd distract her with dinner, let myself get talked into planning fucking happy endings for the agents on my team.

Me.

Planning happy endings.

Yeah, that was the sound of the universe laughing at me.

The screen from the monitor was glowing brightly, making Lily's skin look pale—paler than normal, and I knew that part of that was because of me, because I was an asshole, because I *had* to be an asshole. The rest was because for as bubbly and fun-loving as she was, Lily was one of the hardest workers I had ever met.

Her fingers tapped on the keyboard.

She scrolled. She read.

She kept her gaze fixed on the screen.

My gaze was fixed on her as she worked.

Then on her *and* my watch.

As. She. Worked.

For hours. When she should have been resting. When she should have been decompressing before the mission went down.

Instead, she was glued to the monitor.

And I was getting increasingly more pissed.

The quiet plane at my back. A woman working herself to exhaustion in front of me. Hours ticking by until finally my frustration swelled up inside me and I pushed off the door, striding across the room, leaning over Lily and yanking the plug out of the monitor. "Enough," I growled.

Lily jerked, her head tilting back, her lips parting.

A rare slice of anger flashing through her eyes. "What the fuck, Hannah?" she snapped.

"You need to sleep," I ordered.

"I *need*," she muttered, leaning forward and jamming the plug back into the outlet, "to finish going over these documents."

I let her plug the monitor back in.

Then promptly yanked it back out. "We've reviewed those documents over and over again, baby. There's nothing to look at."

She swiveled the chair to face me. "I need to make sure—"

My fingers wrapped around her wrist, tugged her out of the seat. She stumbled, her body colliding with mine, curves and soft and strength.

A sharp move, pain up my arm.

She broke my grip, tore free.

But I was already moving, pressing her back, stepping

forward, corralling her until she was pinned against the wall and my body.

"Hannah—"

"You're done," I whispered.

She pushed at my shoulders, but I merely grabbed her hands, laced our fingers together, and kept her in place.

"*Hannah.*"

"You're done," I repeated.

Her lips parted, breath shuddering out, heat in her eyes, heat that drew me closer before I even realized it. Until I felt her next shuddering breath on *my* lips.

Until I saw her tongue darting out, moistening her mouth, drawing me in...

Until I was close enough that her scent was in my nose, imprinted on my cells.

Until I leaned even closer and...

I tore myself away.

"No more work," I ordered.

CHAPTER FIVE

LILY

"THREE. TWO. ONE... *GO."*

I moved, slipping around the corner, gun lifted—gaze searching, boots silent on the concrete.

Across the causeway, hidden in the shadows.

Pausing outside the backdoor.

And not a moment too soon.

Because the knob turned, the door slid open, and Ken Rochester slid out into the night.

Gun at his hip, another in his hand. Knife strapped to his right thigh. All mostly hidden by the coat he wore. He was dressed in all black, his hair covered by a tight, dark beanie, but it was definitely Rochester.

One, because the man was a fucking behemoth.

Two, because of the tattoo on his right hand, the edges of it just visible where it gripped the gun, held close to his side so the folds of his coat could hide the weapon as he walked down a public street.

And I supposed it would.

It was late.

The moon was behind clouds.

And people saw what they wanted to see.

I waited until there was enough distance between us so he wouldn't hear and confirmed to the team, "It's him."

"Roger," Hannah said into my ear. "Weapons?"

Quietly, I listed them off.

"Trail at a distance," she ordered. "Watch and backup as necessary."

"On it," I whispered, not much for *rogers*.

Then I trailed and watched.

Watched Linc shift casually into position, striding out of an apartment and getting into a car on the street, prepared to trail by vehicle if necessary. Watched Jesse and Leo play happy couple on the street as a distraction—making out but keeping their awareness in Rochester's direction.

Watched Hannah's back as she stalked him through the shadows.

Her back.

Yeah, I'd been seeing a lot of that lately.

Starting in my office.

Continuing on the plane.

On base. Now—

Focus.

Rochester turned down an alley and I followed my instincts, peeling off from the trailing and watching, and shifting into backup mode.

I'd studied the files, the maps.

I knew the alley appeared to be sealed off.

But it wasn't.

The chain-link fence at the end wasn't bolted. Tenants in the area had complained that teenagers had been vandalizing the area, escaping detection by pushing the metal links to the side and slipping underneath.

I knew that because I'd gone over the reports, the reconnaissance enough times that I *knew*.

So, I moved silently, circling the building.

Seeing the shadows move.

Silent except for the odd scuff of a boot.

Of a *struggle*.

Hannah had closed in.

"Backup. Alley," I said softly into the mic, heard Linc, Leo,
and Jesse confirm they were going in. I moved quickly, effi-
ciently...and got there just in time to hear the rapport of a
silenced bullet hit the building's wall, to hear Hannah's pained
grunt, to hear and see the chain-link move.

Then I sucked in a breath, braced...and...

Moved.

Releasing my breath as I took the brunt of Rochester's weight,
shifted so I moved with his movement, and using a trick that
Hannah had taught me, the same one I'd seen her pull off and
made me fall in love with her, and I slammed him to the ground.

He went down hard, the air knocked out of him.

But he was a former KTS agent.

He might have gone down and done it hard, but he didn't
stay down. He recovered quickly, trying to regain his feet, his
hand going to his hip.

To the gun.

And too fucking close to the knife.

I lurched forward, pinning his wrist, getting one end of a
restraint around it, using my knee, my thigh, my foot to keep
his other from his weapons.

This was to mixed results.

He didn't get the gun out of the holster, but he did manage
to get the knife.

It lanced over my arm, cutting, but not cutting deep because
my clothing was knife- and bullet-resistant. Not cutting deep
because he wasn't aiming for me.

He was aiming...for himself.

Fuck.

I lurched, managed to get my thigh between his knife and his chest, really fucking hating my life when that blade sank— deep because it was close-up, because my pants were knife-resistant, but not knife-*proof*.

They might protect my femoral.

But the fat, the muscle, the skin...not so much.

Plus was, I wouldn't bleed out.

Minus was, it hurt like a bitch.

I twisted, yanked the knife free, pushed it away from my leg. Rochester grunted and bucked, fingers still wrapped around the hilt, but I managed to rip the knife from his grip—this accomplished by breaking his wrist, and considering he'd been trying to choose suicide over disclosing whatever information he might have in his mind, I thought this was a victory.

The blade clattered to the concrete. I ignored the blood, the pain, and flipped him, pressing his face into the street and holding on tight.

Because my team was coming.

Because...then they were there.

Taking over for me, cuffing Rochester—who aside from some pained groans, stayed silent.

I slid back, took stock.

Leg bleeding. Deep. But surprisingly, it wasn't too bad. Painful, but I'd be able to walk on it...with the help of some drugs and some KTS-developed clotting agent (thanks, Olive for inventing it). Arm. More than a scratch, but it might be more problematic. It was near my wrist, and my grip strength felt weak.

Hopefully, the knife hadn't nicked a tendon or something.

And seriously, when the Moldovan Five and the rest of the traitors went down, I was putting all my energy into bullet- and knife-*proof* clothing.

I wasn't a scientist or inventor.

But I could be stubborn as hell and was smart.

I could figure it out.

"Hey, Lil." Linc knelt by my side, pack open, eyes assessing. He was our medic, the one who patched us back together.

"I'm good," I murmured. "Slap a bandage on it, so we can move. We've got to get Rochester back to base."

Linc looked like he wanted to argue.

But we'd all been in on this for a long time, had dealt with the fallout. He knew that whoever was behind the betrayals at KTS had been one step ahead of us the entire time. It was why we needed to move…and why "base" in this case hopefully wasn't going to be the "base" whoever was behind the attacks would expect.

"Okay, Lil," he said. "But we will be having a conversation about using your leg as a pincushion later."

"Couldn't let the fucker stab himself," I muttered, biting back a hiss when he dumped clotting agent on my wound and tied a bandage tightly around my leg.

His brows lifted.

"I don't think he wants us to take him in—"

Alive.

I'd been about to finish that statement with the word *alive*.

Then gunshots rang out.

Not loud like in the movies, but soft *pops* of bullets emerging from barrels covered by silencers, small explosions of brick and concrete and asphalt when those bullets collided with the space around us.

Linc cursed.

I held back *my* curse, unholstered my gun, and we both moved to Hannah, helping her drag Rochester against the wall, seeking cover, searching for the source of the bullets. Luckily, Leo and Jesse had already taken off for the car, so the moment we emerged from the alley, dragging Rochester behind us, the SUV was there, doors thrown open.

Five feet between us and safety.

Five feet that felt like five hundred.

But the longer we waited, the more dangerous it would get. The easier it would be for them to pin us down further.

"Move!" Hannah ordered, sliding to the front of Linc and me, popping out and sending cover fire to the right. Jesse was behind the wheel, Leo providing cover fire the other way.

Linc and I didn't delay.

We hooked our arms under Rochester's and dragged him forward, ignoring his grunt of pain.

Then I was in the SUV, Rochester behind me.

Linc, Hannah, and Leo seconds later.

We took off, skidding away from the sidewalk, flying down the road.

"Any holes?" Hannah asked, turning in her seat as Linc slid into the backseat, eyes coming to mine. "Any *more* holes?" she added softly.

I shook my head.

Linc and Leo replied in the negative.

Rochester—no surprise—said nothing.

CHAPTER SIX

Hannah

I KEPT my gaze on a swivel the entire way to the warehouse, watching for a tail.

Well, for another.

Because we'd *had* a tail.

But Jess was a good driver.

She'd lost it, and then we'd traded vehicles. Broke into two groups. Linc and Lily in one. Me, Jess, Rochester, and Leo in the other.

Better to split up.

Better to keep more eyes on the road.

Better to reconvene from two separate locations.

Now Jess had sprinted to the roll-up door, both cars slid inside, and she yanked the door down behind them.

The engines went off.

We piled out of the cars.

Leo staying with Rochester.

The rest of us clearing and making certain the building was secure. The rest of us minus Lily, who had blood-slicked clothing on and was limping. "Sit the fuck down," I hissed, grabbing her arm and forcing her into one of the few chairs that were present in the space.

"I'm fine," she hissed back, shaking me off and proceeding to her preassigned quadrant.

Limping.

Blood stains on her sleeve, her hand, all down her leg.

I wanted to argue, but we needed to lock this place down. We needed to get information out of Rochester. We needed to flush out the traitors, locate and eradicate the human traffickers, the drug dealers, the bad guys.

We needed to go back to what we did best.

Saving the fucking world.

And that couldn't happen until the moles were ferreted out, until men like the fucker that Leo was strapping to the chair had their power stripped from them.

Which meant we needed to know how far the rot went.

My phone buzzed, and I finished clearing my section of the warehouse before taking out my cell, checking to see that it was a message from Laila.

They'd taken their target into custody and were beginning interrogation.

Still no word from Jeff or Skye.

That had a sick pit opening in my stomach, but I didn't have control over those missions, didn't dare reach out until they initiated contact for fear of jeopardizing the overall mission.

Instead, I needed to focus on the interrogation.

Not on the fact that I might fail to get any pertinent information. Not on Lily and the blood dripping down her hand, her leg.

Not on anything except trying to get one piece of intel that we could use to move forward.

Another buzz.

Skye checking in.

They and their target were secure.

Now just waiting on Jeff.

Lily came back into the space, trailed by Linc and Jesse. They spoke softly then took up positions around the area, Leo backing away from Rochester and joining them in keeping watch.

And effectively leaving the former KTS agent with me.

I smiled.

Thought about Lily bleeding. About the kids and women we hadn't been able to save from the traffickers. About the agents who'd been wounded and killed, put at risk, sources compromised. Missions fucked.

My mind narrowed to the task at hand.

I knew my team had my back.

But I also knew that I couldn't wait to get information out of Ken Rochester, willingly...or motivated by the sharp tip of my blade.

The first might be faster.

The second would be more fun.

———

INTERROGATION WAS EXHAUSTING WORK.

Blood dripped down Rochester's legs, his arms, his face, pooled on the concrete beneath his chair.

Payback for Lily, not that I would admit that.

But also because...he wasn't particularly motivated to talk.

And we were running out of time.

Close to twelve hours had passed, twelve hours of keeping him awake, asking him the same questions in different ways, hoping to trip him up, trying to get beyond the training KTS had ingrained in all of us agents.

One piece of information.

God, we just needed *one* piece.

But it was fucking difficult to interrogate someone who had

no fear of me, who wasn't afraid to die, who wasn't worried about being killed, slowly, painfully...by inches.

Lily strode over.

No. *Limped*.

Linc had looked her over, finished treating the wounds, removed the field dressing from her thigh, and took care of her in a way that I knew she'd be up and back to normal sooner rather than later, and not just because of the special healing compound he'd used liberally. But because Linc had done a thorough job, because he would keep an eye on it. Because I had, too, even as I worked.

But I knew that even though she was tough as hell, she had to be feeling it because she'd still used herself as a fucking pincushion. Putting her leg in the way of that blade, using her own flesh to stop Rochester from killing himself.

Putting *herself* at risk.

Fury pumped through my veins at the thought of Lily hurting herself.

Working too hard. Not sleeping enough. Not eating right.

Letting herself be that fucking pincushion.

Fuck.

I gritted my teeth, forced myself to hold tight to my shit, as she came close, as the soft scent of her filled my senses, as yearning mixed with fury and need filled every single one of my cells to near-bursting.

I shoved it down, ignored the fact that it was getting harder every time I pushed back the urge to make a go of it with her, to take what I wanted.

Desperately.

But I was good at pretending I didn't feel anything, good at ignoring the draw to her.

Good at stopping myself from longing for things I couldn't have.

Things I was too broken to have.

How did I give love when I didn't know how? How did I accept it when no one had thought me worthy of it?

Lily does.

That thought was a gut punch, because she'd said those words in her office, because I'd felt them deeply even as I threw up barriers and ice and got the fuck out.

But circling back to being too broken.

To accept it. To give her what she deserved, what she needed.

I wouldn't do that to her.

I *couldn't.*

So, I locked that shit down, buried it deep underground, and I did what I did best: focused on work.

Lil's gaze hit mine, and I knew, *knew* she wanted me to let her take over. And I *knew* that every bone in my body, no, every fiber, every *cell* revolted at the notion of Lily being anywhere near that fucking monster strapped to the chair.

Or maybe the monster was me?

Since I was the one who'd strapped him down. Who'd made him bleed, who had broken his other arm without a trace of remorse. Who wouldn't lose one ounce of sleep over torturing the fucker, not if it meant the betrayals at KTS would stop, not if it meant that we could get back to saving the world.

Not if it meant that I'd been able to return some of the pain he'd given to Lily.

All of it.

Multiplied by a hundred.

She strode past me without hesitation, sliding her gaze away, knowing that even as protective of my team as I was—because I was *always* protective my team, had the back of the people who had *my* back—that I wouldn't ever diminish my teammates' abilities.

That I wouldn't stop them from doing something they were good at.

I'd curb the protective urges.

I would let them do their job.

Because they *were* good at it. *Lily* was good at it—really *fucking* good at interrogations, soft and gentle when she went in to get the information, sometimes coaxing it free without the target even knowing it happened.

I just needed to remember that.

And continue to curb the protective urges, especially the ones that had me wanting to yank Lily behind me, or to bundle her off someplace safe.

Except, there *wasn't* a place that was one hundred percent safe. There *wouldn't* be.

Not until this business was done.

So, I bit my tongue, let Lily move by me.

Limp by me, dragging a chair, the metal scraping loudly against the concrete floor. I didn't help her, didn't throw myself bodily in between them—and yeah, I was having a few issues with keeping my distance, keeping things strictly professional...

But she was my friend.

It was natural to be concerned about my friend.

My. Friend.

Fucking liar.

And seriously, I did *not* need my inner voice fucking with my head.

Lock it down. Focus on the now.

Which I did by backing into the shadows, taking over Lily's quadrant of the watch, and letting her have the space to work.

"What happened in Berlin, Kenny?" she asked softly.

Silkily.

Dangerously, but Rochester didn't know that, didn't understand that soft and silky could be dangerous. He was used to brute force. He *wasn't* used to gentle questions and pretty brown eyes. He wasn't used to someone who did as much research as Lily obviously had.

Because I didn't know anything about Berlin.

But Lily did, clearly.

And it meant something to Rochester, and paired with her use of *Kenny*, had focus entering his gaze for the first time in hours. I watched him drop back into his body, pain entering his eyes.

Not all physical either.

Lily was on to something with Berlin.

So, I watched, waited, listened, felt the air around the warehouse grow taut. From Rochester, from Leo, Linc, and Jesse.

They'd seen it, felt it, too.

"Don't say a fucking word about it," Rochester snapped.

"About Amy?" Lily said softly.

He growled, spitting blood.

And I felt a smile curve my lips.

Because Lily was good. *Fucking* good. Because she'd found it, the motivation, the trigger, the piece that would get us a grain of information.

"Is she safe?" she whispered. "I can help you get her safe."

Rochester went still, then he began lurching at the bonds, seemingly ignoring the broken bones as he fought against the restraints. "Don't fucking talk about her. Don't think about her. Don't say her goddamned name, you fucking bitch."

I straightened off the pillar I'd leaned against.

Lily didn't stop the quiet, the soft, wasn't cowed by the rage on Rochester's face.

"She won't ever be safe, Kenny," she said. "Not with the group out there. Not with the trafficking and the attacks on KTS."

Then Lily dropped the bomb.

"Your daughter will *never* be safe unless you help us stop these men."

CHAPTER SEVEN

LILY

I KNEW I had him when his eyes slid closed, when he stopped fighting against the restraints.

"I can get your daughter safe," I said gently.

His head snapped up, eyes blazing. "No, you fucking can't. These people—"

He cut himself off.

I waited.

For more.

For him to give us *something*, anything.

When he didn't, I kept turning the screws. "You help us," I said softly. "You help us take down those behind the attacks, and we'll be able to make sure she's safe. Safe *forever*," I added when a muscle in his jaw ticked. "Not safe and hidden away, keeping your distance from her and hoping that they won't find your daughter." I leaned closer. "If I found her, you know they have, too."

That had him going still.

"I'm good at my job," I whispered. "You know that. You

know that's why I'm here and you're"—I nodded at the chair
—"*there*. But you also know that they've been one step ahead
of us this entire time. So, if I know about your adorable,
blond-haired, blue-eyed daughter who at six loves watching
makeup tutorials on YouTube and asked for a makeup kit for
Christmas last year, then you know—*you know*—they know it,
too."

Still, *so* still.

"So, help me," I said, still whispering. "Help me do my job.
Help me get her safe, *keep* her safe. Help me help all of the other
little girls who love makeup and YouTube and are missing their
dads be safe. Help me find those who *aren't* so we can *get* them
safe."

Silence.

Then his shoulders slumped.

And then I had him. All the way.

His eyes met mine.

"You get her. You get her safe. And then I'll talk."

I was shaking my head even before he finished. "No, Kenny.
You have to give me something first. Make it big. Make it
important." His lips parted, protest forming on his face. "But
keep something back, keep some collateral. I'll understand,
honey. You know I will."

He inhaled.

Then let me have it.

Or *some* of it, anyway…

"They're called the Confederate."

Stupid fucking name, I thought, but I didn't say that, just
asked, "Who's in charge?"

A shake of his head. "I don't know. They don't use names.
Aside from me, Daniel, Steve, Matt, and Laura, I don't know the
identities of anyone involved in the operation. They find collateral on you. They *use* collateral on you. You don't question it, or
that collateral ends up dead."

"Why you five?"

Another jump of that muscle in his jaw. "Because that mission in Moldova was fucked."

Slowly, I leaned back in my chair. "The mission report didn't say it was fucked."

His eyes flickered. "It was fucked. Trust me, it was *really* fucked. Seriously fucked."

I lifted my brows, waited for him to give it to me.

"We didn't accomplish the objective. Not even close. Civilians died. Matt...he...the injury that took him out was from Daniel's bullet. Not from a fall. It was friendly fire, and he almost didn't make it out."

I inhaled slowly.

I knew the report.

I'd *read* the report a dozen times, knew there was nothing in it that even hinted at a mission gone FUBAR. And those reports had to be supported by evidence, signed off by the whole team, and then superiors had to clear that evidence to sign off on the report. It wasn't easy to falsify, not with so many moving parts, security footage, the video feeds from KTS base monitoring the mission, or hell, even the film that was pulled from body cams.

For something that big—friendly fire to dead civilians—that was seemingly impossible to have happened.

Yet it had.

And there were other reports that had been falsified.

Not to that extent that I knew.

But we'd found inconsistencies.

"Contact is online or strictly on burners," Kenny said. "One in-person visit was enough. They had pictures...I'd hidden her, but she was...*they* were..."

"What's their objective?" I asked softly after he'd trailed off, waiting for him to finish and not getting that finish, not getting more.

His eyes shot to mine. "You get her. You get her safe, and I'll tell you the rest."

I felt Hannah shift, knew she was unhappy with him giving

orders. My body was always attuned to hers, with every single movement she made, but I didn't break eye contact with Kenny, just agreed. "Okay."

And felt Hannah stiffen further. She didn't like that.

But Kenny had given.

We needed to as well.

Not to mention the man had two broken arms, blood dripping down his face, his limbs. It was a fucking miracle he was conscious...

So, I'd give on this.

And maybe—probably—when he was closer to *un*conscious, I'd push again.

Work smarter, not harder.

Also, this just in, I might look like a nice person on the outside, but I could be ruthless, I could be a bitch. I was a fucking secret agent, and I'd do anything to protect KTS, to protect the innocents I put my life on the line for.

Kenny's eyes had shot to mine, hope blooming in the blue depths. "Okay?"

A nod.

"You give us the info. We'll pick her up. While we do that, you give me more. Then you give everything you have when she gets here. After that, the two of you go, get the fuck away. Hide and hide deep until this shit is *done*."

"I—"

My leg fucking hurt. My arm, wrist, and fingers didn't feel much better.

I wanted information.

I wanted this done.

I—

He said, "I tracked one of their IP addresses."

My eyes lifted, met Hannah's. She nodded.

"Tell me where your daughter is." A beat. "And then tell me more."

He told me where his daughter was.

He told me more.

And then we got to fucking work.

———

JEFF'S TEAM WAS SAFE.

Their target was dead, having gone down in a shoot-out that meant Jeff's team was lucky to get out safe.

Skye and Laila hadn't yet found the pins to push to move their targets.

Leo and Jesse had slipped out of the warehouse to retrieve Amy. Meanwhile, Linc, Hannah, and I had taken Kenny and gone to a hotel.

A reservation under a false name.

A random woman on the street paid to check in and retrieve the key, who was smoke the moment she got that hundred-euro bill.

We used the service entrance.

Avoiding cameras.

All this to hopefully avoid the Confederate.

Linc saw to me, stitching me up and using more of the clotting agent and bandages and pain relief. Then Linc saw to Kenny. Setting his broken bones, strapping them with braces and patching him up.

And all the while, I talked, followed by him talking.

And as he did, Hannah took notes and researched.

Until Kenny passed out.

Until *I* passed out.

Until warm fingers brushed over my forehead, and I realized that I'd passed out. Hannah sat on the edge of the bed; her eyes locked onto mine.

"My turn for watch?" I asked, sitting up and biting back a wince.

She pressed my shoulder, lightly nudging me back into the mattress. "Linc's on it."

I glanced over, saw that Linc was, indeed, on it.

Then glanced over, saw that Kenny was restrained on the floor between the bed and window with the drapes shut tight.

Because he might be working with us, might have given us collateral to potentially use against him during a time when trust was a slender thread, but we weren't stupid. We hadn't gotten this far by trusting. Hell, we'd only gotten this far because we'd *stopped* trusting.

Started second-guessing everything.

Old missions. Old friends and connections.

Working our way through everyone—from me outward. To Hannah. To our team. To Laila's team. Then Jeff and Skye's.

And they'd all done the same.

Now we had a small group we could trust, and we could get some fucking work done.

But Hannah didn't have her laptop. In fact, it was closed and sitting on the desk.

Which begged the question...why?

Had the work stalled when I fell asleep?

Did I need to rouse that fucker—because Kenny *was* a fucker who'd betrayed KTS—and get more information than I had before he'd been hopped up on morphine—coincidentally *not* the pain pills that Linc had given me the night before? See? I was totally ruthless. I'd take advantage of Kenny being loopy from morphine.

I had.

No regrets.

Also, side note, yes, I understood why Kenny betrayed us, why he'd played the part he had (or what little of that part I understood so far), but he was still a fucker. He had still betrayed us.

So, yeah, I got it.

I didn't forget his daughter had been in the crosshairs.

But he could have handled this differently. He could have

found a way to make it so he didn't betray everything we worked for.

People had died. Good agents. Innocent civilians.

Lives were changed forever, families torn apart.

Bodies had been broken.

And he'd helped that along.

"What's up?" I asked, pushing to sitting again, reaching for the bottle of water, those pain pills that Linc had left out for me, flexing my fingers, feeling the healing skin there go taut. It hurt, but not terribly. Mostly because Linc did good work, but also because paired with the healing component of the clotting agent, the couple of hours of sleep, and I felt like a million bucks.

Well, maybe twenty-five thousand.

Stiff. Like I'd been stabbed.

But alive and with information and hopefully several steps closer to taking down the Confederate. They were smart and covered their tracks. Had apparently planned this for a long while before they even began making moves.

Having moles at KTS, financing from selling drugs, selling flesh.

Dirt on agents. Positions of power in other organizations, in governments that made it easy for them to move across borders. Working in the shadows, access to tech.

Sneaky. As. Fuck.

All of this made it hard as hell for us to track them.

But, finally, progress.

And it was that progress I was focused on when I started to shift off the bed.

"He's out," Hannah said. "Leo and Jesse are on the kid. We have nothing to do at this point but to wait and plan."

Yeah. That planning part was why I needed to get my ass in gear.

I stood up.

"Rest," Hannah ordered, shoving me back down.

"I need to get to work," I said. "Research what he gave us—"

"It's done."

Said like everything *was* said and done.

Like there wasn't any other information I might dig up and—

I sat up. "I need to look—"

A firm hand on my shoulder. "You *need* to rest."

"Hannah, *I need* to work…" I shoved her off, found my feet, striding over to my computer.

One second my fingers were grazing my laptop, the next, a hand was wrapped tight around my arm, firm pressure dragging me away from the desk, away from the bed, and into the bathroom.

The door *clicked* closed.

Hannah's body pressed to mine.

Her mouth descended.

CHAPTER EIGHT

Hannah

WIDE BROWN EYES ON MINE.

"What the fuck are you playing at?" I hissed.

Lily jerked back, her eyes going wider. And fuck, but she had the prettiest eyes I'd ever seen. Dark, dark chocolate that had need coursing through me. I wanted to watch them darken with desire. I wanted to study the specks of gold that were like sunshine or the glimmer of fool's gold on a beach. Not overtly obvious, but when the daylight hit just right, that sparkle just exploded all around.

Turned mundane into something beautiful.

Turned beautiful into soul-shattering.

Turned—

She shoved me back. *Hard.* "What the fuck?"

All that beauty and soul-alteration disappeared, and *my* fury exploded.

But apparently, she was even more furious because when I reached for her, she executed a move that was all kinds of dirty and all kinds of effective, seeing as I found myself with my front shoved against the wall, her body pinning mine. The only reason I didn't end up with a bloody (or broken) nose being *I'd* taught her that move that was all sorts of dirty.

As thus, even though I'd been taken by surprise, because I'd taught her those tricks, I didn't end up with blood pouring down my face.

Go me.

Go *her*.

Because, fuck, if her body didn't feel freaking perfect against mine. Fuck, if it didn't make me want what I couldn't have. Fuck, if it didn't—

Make me burn, make me want, make me…*yearn*.

Which was something I really couldn't be doing considering we had a hot target in the other room, a team member on watch and supervising that target.

And a heart that was filled with quicksand.

If I took one step forward, it would suck her down, fill her mouth, her nose, her ears, her eyes with the rough granules. Packing tight, clogging her airways, choking her, snuffing out her life until…until—

She let me go.

Her chest was heaving, and she was holding her injured arm gingerly, pain edging into those sparkles of sunshine in her eyes.

Hurting.

Because of me.

Quicksand sucking her under, snuffing her out.

Until the glimmer of beauty would disappear, and disappointment would shine out, and—

I'd lose her.

She leaned in as I spun around, and, for a second, her lips were so close to mine that I could taste her lip gloss.

Peppermint. This time she tasted like peppermint.

Then she jabbed a finger into my chest. "I *have* to work."

A hiss. A demand. A…plea to leave her alone.

I couldn't.

"You're injured."

There.

Just beyond the glimmer. Just dipping a finger into tempered chocolate, slowly dragging it across cool granite.

A softness appearing that was so fucking dangerous. Because it stole my breath and made me want...and because it made me remember why I couldn't.

"I *have* to work," she said again. No less of a plea. No less devastating to everything inside me.

"You *need*—"

One finger gliding across my bottom lip.

Not soft. The tip was calloused from years of training. And then the touch wasn't soft either, that finger pressing in against my lips, dipping into my mouth.

Unbidden, my tongue flicked out.

Tasted...

Lily.

Flowers and sweet. Capable and strong. Everything I'd ever wanted and knew I couldn't have.

Her lips parted, air slicing out, and we were close enough that I felt that breath on my skin. Tingles slid down my spine when I thought of the other places I might feel that burst of hot, silken air.

As she kissed down my neck.

Between my breasts.

Joined by that roughened fingertip in skating over my nipples.

Farther. Along my stomach, my belly button, one hip bone and then the other.

Changing directions and skipping over my pussy, because I knew—I *knew* Lily would be a tease. Leaving that for last because it would be worth the pleasurable torture, because I'd be so fucking wet that I'd be desperate for her tongue, her fingers.

And because she was Lily, because she was sweet and soft and giving, that tease wouldn't last long, wouldn't be to torture me. It would be just long enough that it would ramp the need, drive me crazy in the best possible way before she would move between my thighs.

Drag her tongue higher.

Delicate circles, complicated patterns, the odd nibble to make me jump.

My legs spreading wider.

Her mouth moving closer—

"*Don't.*"

I blinked.

The fantasy disappearing in that opening and closing of my lids. A heartbeat passed, and I was back in the bathroom, the harsh fluorescents making both of us look pale and tired...

Or maybe that was just Lily, since she was blocking my reflection in the mirror.

Because she was pale and tired and...*determined*.

"You made it clear you don't want this," she said.

No. *Snapped.* In the same tone as her *don't* from a few seconds before. Lily. *My* Lily was snapping. My sunshine and glimmer and soft and sweet was snapping.

Because of me.

Quicksand.

Fuck. I didn't want that. I couldn't see her like that.

But I also couldn't do that to her. Couldn't—

"You don't want to go there," she said, molten ore instead of sunshine in her gaze. "Fine. I got that. But this"—she waved a hand between our bodies, and swear to fucking God, everywhere from my breasts to toes—and in between—tingled—"*this* cannot happen. I love you, Hannah. I have for years. Full stop."

I sucked in a breath.

Those words washing over me.

Changing everything...and changing nothing.

"Us not going there because you don't want it? Also, fine.

However," she said fiercely, stepping back, crossing her arms, putting distance between us that I seriously did *not* like, even though I understood and clung tightly to it all the same. "*However*, not going there means you need to be my team leader. Just my team leader. Not my concerned friend. Not a partner I want in my bed and my life—and not just my work life."

More breath sucking, more terror slicing through my insides. More need tearing me up.

Her arms relaxed, dropping to her sides, a sad little smile on her lips. "I see that freaks you out. I *get* why it does, probably more than anyone."

Because I'd shared.

Not everything.

But enough that she knew why I drew a hard line at friendship.

Always.

Even if that line kept getting smudged when it came to Lily.

Smudged. Erased. Blurred. *Fucked.*

"Lil," I began.

"Lily," she corrected. "Just Lily. Your team member. Your second in command. Your friend." She surprised the shit out of me by stepping forward, pressing the front of her body to mine. Hands lifting and cupping my jaw. Her chin lifting and our lips aligning. A brush. Once. Twice.

I opened my mouth, wanting more.

Wanting her tongue dancing against mine. Her hands roving my skin. Our breaths exchanged as the kiss exploded. Our bodies in sync. Clothing on the floor. My fingers between her thighs, finding her wet and—

She leaned further, mouth coming to my ear. "But just that, Hannah. Friends. Teammates. You give the orders. I follow—but only if they don't come from that fucked-up place in your head. The one that strives to keep punishing yourself, to take from you time and again. Because, yeah, your parents fucked with you. Because they were horrible assholes who damaged the wonderful woman in your heart and mind. But also because you *let* them keep doing it, keep fucking with you." She straightened, eyes hitting mine. "You think you deserve this punishment."

Everything inside me arrested. Froze.

As those words hit home.

Struck deep…and true.

A glint in those chocolate depths, and I braced even before I heard the rest of her words.

Because I knew it was going to slice, and it would be even deeper than the previous words.

"And maybe you *do* deserve it," she whispered. "Maybe when a person spends so long punishing herself for something that isn't—and wasn't *ever*—in their control, maybe when they have good people around them who love them and want more for them, even though they do their best to push them away, maybe when they have a path that could lead to a boatload of happy and it just requires *one* step forward—one *fucking* step!— and they're too much of a coward to inch forward…maybe they deserve that punishment."

My throat went tight.

Agony sliced through me.

"Because *they* think they deserve it," she finished quietly, hitting that final nail, tapping it home, sealing the wooden lid tight overhead. "Because no matter what you say and do otherwise, they'll keep punishing themselves. Over and over and *over* again. Shoring their heart in concrete, until your fingernails are bloody and broken from trying to break through, and the moment you do… The *moment* you get a glimpse of that beauty inside, they're smoothing on another layer from the inside, ensuring that all that bleeding, all that pain and effort and determination to get them to see, to come out, to love you back enough to want more…all of that means nothing. Absolutely fucking *nothing*."

I *was* bloody and broken...and encased in concrete.

Because the bloody and broken on *my* nails were from furiously skimming on layer after layer, from building it up, making certain the holes that Lil made were covered.

Because *inside*...I was bloody and broken, too.

And I could never *ever* let someone in to see it.

CHAPTER NINE

LILY

I LAY ON THE BED, gaze on the ceiling, laptop closed next to me, listening to the various parties in the room breathe.

Counting each inhale and exhale. Tallying the breaths per hour in my mind. Keeping a mental checklist of who was asleep, who was faking sleep, and who wasn't bothering.

Because it was better than the guilt that was tearing me up inside.

I'd told her she deserved it.

Deserved. *It.*

Deserved the parents who beat and disowned her, leaving her alone and scarred to the very center of her being.

I'd told her she deserved *that.*

And I'd told her she deserved the things I didn't know about. The dark, barbed memories jabbing at her soul that she hadn't been able to tell me about because I knew, instinctively, they were so much worse than shitty parents and a mental health crisis and cry for help—all of which had brought her so much agony, so much torment that Hannah, *my* Hannah who was so fucking strong and untouchable, had cried.

Not much. Maybe six tears.

But she'd cried.

And I'd told her eight hours before that she deserved it.

When she had a soul that was so good, it should be bronzed and hung on the walls near the pearly gates.

A soul that sure as fuck didn't deserve being punished.

Despite me telling her that.

Which meant that *I* needed to be punished.

Sigh.

Hannah—the only one who was actually asleep. On the floor because she'd refused to sleep on the bed, what with my injuries.

Considering they hurt like fuck—though the hurt like fuck was of healing injuries thanks to the special compound Olive had invented and Linc had applied copiously to my wounds—I hadn't argued over taking the bed.

One, it was more comfortable.

Two, I was done arguing with Hannah for the foreseeable future.

Three—

There wasn't a three.

I'd come out of the bathroom, worked while Hannah took over Linc's watch and Linc got some much-needed shuteye. Then I'd taken *my* turn at watch while Linc slipped out for food, during which Hannah and Kenny had slept (the former faking it, the latter, with injuries worse than my own and his body needing it, actually sleeping).

Jesse and Leo had reported in and were en route.

Which meant when Kenny had woken up to word of his daughter being transported to the safe house, he'd gotten talkative.

More details—details that were fed to Laila and Skye's teams to use in the interrogations (that weren't going well because we still didn't have any lynchpins to pull when it came to the final two members of the Moldovan Five), and a few that were fed to Jeff's team so they could keep investigating.

We were on the Confederate, though.

That was strictly between our team and no one else, and we were doing our damndest to keep that shit locked down.

Because we needed to go slow and steady.

Because we needed Kenny and Amy to stay alive, to stash them someplace safe, and to get anything else we could out of him.

Then we would move careful and smart and—

Not tear our teammates to shreds with venom in our words and the fucking world on the line.

Fuck.

I slowly straightened up in bed, feeling my thigh pull and itch—a good sign. My wrist was sore, especially when I positioned my computer in my lap and started reviewing the notes I'd made.

Specifically, the ones to do with the tattoo parlor in Berlin where Kenny had gotten inked.

It was oddly positioned, because there was one thing that didn't belong on the otherwise seedy-looking intersection of old winding streets.

Bars.

Tattoo parlors.

Strip clubs.

Bars. (Yes, it bore repeating, considering the quantity of liquor establishments in the four-block radius I was looking at).

And...a church.

Old, rundown, totally unlisted everywhere—in fact, it looked like an ancient apartment building—except that it had been featured on a blogger's website about hidden gems because of the exquisite woodwork and stained glass inside.

"I think the doors were supposed to be locked, but I happened to notice that the door wasn't latched and caught a glimpse of a ceremony

taking place behind the heavy oak panels. Music and incense and stained glass and gold. I couldn't resist slipping inside, standing at the back, and observing."

My eyes skimmed beyond the descriptions of stained glass and perfectly carved wooden cherubs.

To a paragraph that had my nape prickling.

I moved on silent feet to an empty pew at the back, quietly observing the men and women moving up the aisles toward the altar, placing various offerings on a large, gilded platter. Money and small boxes, jewelry and packages that were wrapped tightly in brown paper. I didn't realize that each row was going until a man arrived at my pew, extended a hand marked with a beautiful tattoo of moon and scales toward the altar, and said, 'Quod vero dicitur per comparationem.'

Prickling had been replaced by phantom fingers, squeezing tight, warning me to pay attention.

Of course, I was *already* paying attention.

I didn't need those phantom fingers.

Quod vero dicitur per comparationem.

The truth is relative.

The words that were tattooed on Kenny's hand. The words that had been tattooed on Daniel's, on the person who'd broken into the KTS base in Atlanta and murdered him. The tattoos that adorned the skin of the Moldovan Five.

The truth is relative.

The truth...

What truth?

And *how* was it relative? Because this wasn't a story being spun. This was murder and drugs and human trafficking. Ruining lives and slavery.

Horrible.

There was no *relative* that could ever make that right.

My eyes slid down on the screen, reading the girl's account. How she'd tried to demure the offering, but the man had grabbed her arm and dragged her from the pew. How she'd stopped fighting to remain an observer and how she'd walked up the aisle, digging her hand into her jacket pocket and pulling out the only offering she had.

A few bills and coins.

Then she'd tried to slip out of the church, found the doors locked.

I admit I got a little nervous here. But I'd come this far, so I decided to sit back down into the pew and wait for the ceremony to be over. Luckily, since I was in the final pew, it didn't take much longer. A priest in a heavy gray and red robe, the hood folded and laying across broad shoulders, his face beautiful, had been joined by a woman. They'd spoken in German, words I couldn't discern, but somehow still beautiful in the strong, staccato language. Candles were lit. Heads bowed. Silence observed. And then at a quiet word, the ceremony was over. Heads coming back up, candles being blown out, soft conversations began. I waited by the doors until they were unlocked, and then they were held wide for me to exit, the same tattooed man from the pew now smiling at me. Smiling back at him, I lifted my phone, snapped one more picture of the gorgeous interior, and then I slipped out into the night air and prepared to do what I did best: party the night away.

There was room for photos below that paragraph, and though several loaded (of an intricate pattern carved into the top of the pew, of a small stained-glass window of St. George, of the gilded edges of a bible), several more didn't, including one that had the description: *Interior of church. Note the large altar laid with offerings.*

The next post was filled with images of cocktails and flirting with a sexy German before dancing the night away.

Then one of her in Copenhagen, doing much of the same—a little sightseeing, a lot of drinking and partying and dancing.

I kept clicking, finding more of the same in new destinations.

Stockholm.

Prague.

Milan.

Paris.

And then I bit back a curse.

Paris was the last post.

Well, the last written by the blogger. Because the final post on her website was written by the girl's family. Saying they were saddened to report that she'd passed away.

Dead.

After visiting a church.

A blog post left in place, but innocuous and not showing anything unless you knew what you were looking for. Pictures mostly intact—minus the ones that actually showed anything pertinent.

And a reasonable amount of time passing before…

I did more research, tracked the blogger through social media and the AP and foreign presses, and found what I was looking for.

Influencer and blogger Wendy Travels was found dead in her hotel room in London last night. The toxicology report is ongoing, but all signs point to an overdose.

In London.

Where KTS had a base.

Along with Berlin, Copenhagen, Stockholm, Prague, Milan, *and* Paris.

Easy to track, to wait and watch and plan for the perfect moment so that no suspicions would blow back onto the Confederate.

But why keep the church post up?

I dug further, found the answer deep in *Wendy Travels* social media page.

A picture of those doors that hadn't latched, enough of the surrounding buildings so it would be easy to find.

Posted before she'd gone in.

With a quippy caption to come find her if she went missing (which had probably been funny to her at the time but wasn't the least bit funny to me considering that I knew how the

Confederate worked) and that her blog post would be up later that night.

So, that post had gone up.

Millions had seen it.

Which meant that it wouldn't be easy to eliminate her without notice.

And the Confederate had survived this long because they operated without extra attention.

So, waiting for it to go up, altering it to stop it from incriminating anything by making certain the pictures didn't load, that the text didn't give away anything sensitive, tracking *Wendy Travels* throughout her trip...

And then when the opportunity presented itself, making her disappear.

Which begged the question, who else had they made disappear?

It was a question I knew I would never get answered.

CHAPTER TEN

Hannah

ROCHESTER WAS VERTICAL.

Both arms were splinted, but I didn't give a fuck that the man wouldn't be able to wipe his own ass—discovered when Linc escorted him into the bathroom and had the joyous gift of watching him do his business.

Another moment to be thankful for not having a dick.

Not having to see *Rochester's* dick.

He was also bruised, scabbed over, and limping ten times worse than Lily was.

Mostly because I hadn't let Linc use the healing agent Olive had invented on Rochester.

He was a former KTS agent, so it would be easier to keep watch on him if he wasn't fully mobile (*and* if those arms weren't up for hand-to-hand combat, holding guns—or *knives*, I thought, glaring at him as he hobbled his way into the back of our rental car).

Jesse and Leo had found a safe house in Greece and were proceeding straight there.

We were taking a more circuitous route and would arrive hopefully a day after them.

Phone calls had been made, Rochester speaking to his daughter, and luckily my heart was surrounded in all that concrete, my efforts to patch up any cracks successful, otherwise the emotion in his voice, the tears gathering in Lily's eyes when she looked away would have had me blubbering like an idiot.

I glanced down at my fingernails, half expecting them to be bloodied and cracked.

They weren't, of course.

And, *of course*, I hadn't blubbered at the conversation conducted on speaker between father and daughter, the former relieved to hear her voice, the latter excited for the adventure and her new friends (thank fuck Jesse and Leo were good with kids) and finally being able to see her dad in person again.

Which, apparently, hadn't happened for nine months.

Nine. Months.

Fuck, the Confederate were dirty.

Keeping a seven-year-old from her father for almost a year?

Yes, I knew that was far from the worst thing they'd done. It just...fuck, Rochester loved her, and if a traitor like him could love his daughter—

Don't.

It didn't matter that the word rocketed through my brain like a whip.

The thoughts still came.

Rochester was a murderer, a traitor, a coward...and he still loved his daughter.

So why couldn't my parents love me?

Don't.

This time the word wasn't whipping across my psyche. This time I was thinking it. Because I didn't need to be in my fucking head and thinking about the past, and worrying about nothing, and—

"Focus, Hannah," I muttered under my breath, forcing myself to check our surroundings one more time before slipping behind the wheel. The engine was on, Lily was in the front passenger seat, Linc and Rochester were in the back.

We all had on facial prosthetics, wigs, hats, and clothing that deliberately changed body shape.

We were parked in a space that had been cleared of cameras, had checked and rechecked clothing, wigs, and hats, the car, our weapons and electronics for trackers and bugs and anything that might compromise the safe house.

We had a route planned—and several backup tracks—along with multiple vehicle switches (some set up as diversions just in case, others planned to be used, others reserved as backup).

Driving in shifts. Watching for tails.

It was going to be a long forty-eight hours.

But we'd get Rochester there. We'd make sure he and his daughter were secure. We'd get the last bit of information he was holding back.

And then he was on his own.

I put the car into drive, and we took off for Greece under the cover of night.

———

LILY WAS DRIVING.

I was cramming fries in my mouth as quickly as possible.

Because…potatoes.

Because…fried potatoes and ketchup.

If I were encased in concrete with bloody fucking finger-nails, the least I could do was wash up and enjoy some potatoes —or rather some potatoes *with* my ketchup.

Not any of that off-brand stuff either.

Heinz only.

I wanted those fifty-seven varieties of tomatoes, vinegar, sugar, and a dash of salt.

I *wanted* to focus on those fifty-seven varieties because Rochester was asleep, Linc was taking watch, and I was wolfing down calories before I was taking a nap. Then I'd be on Rochester duty while Linc drove and Lily ate and slept.

Rotating straight four-hour shifts.

Halfway to Greece.

Three car changes, twenty-four hours on the road, multiple countries, too much fast food and gas station treats, and arriving at the safe house in Greece hopefully just after midnight that night.

Leo and Jesse had checked in.

Amy's hair had been dyed, cut, her wardrobe changed.

They were as safe as—

Eyes flicking to the rearview, Lily changed lanes.

I dropped my ketchup (and the container with a few fry crumbs remaining) into the bag, pulled out my gun. "What?"

A shake of her head, gaze on the road then on the mirror again. "Black sedan, six cars back."

She changed lanes again, and I studied the passenger-side mirror as she took an exit, slid through the signal, and got back on the highway, this time going the other direction.

We got back on the freeway just in time to see the black sedan exit.

"Fuck," I hissed.

Two miles to the next exit.

Lily pulled over to the fast lane, gunned it, put some distance between us and the on-ramp. I spun in my seat, watched Linc do the same, our eyes glued to the road behind us. All the while, the exit grew nearer.

The black sedan entered the highway, headlights coming up fast enough that I knew its driver had floored it as well.

The exit was just a mile ahead.

Lily wove through the cars going the speed limit like they were standing still.

Then the exit was three-quarters of a mile ahead, and she was still weaving, the black sedan growing closer.

Then one half a mile ahead. The headlights, the sedan was six car lengths behind.

Then one-quarter—

"Go!" I ordered.

Lily accelerated, jumping across traffic and sliding the car into a tiny spot between two big rigs that were puttering along in the second lane.

Then pulled over another lane and hit the brakes.

The sudden deceleration meant the sedan had to brake, too.

Right as we reached the off-ramp.

Right as the big rigs covered our movements.

I heard the squealing of tires, the sedan slowing down hard as it tried to make the exit. Then held my breath as Lily sped again, slipped back into that gap, and then over once more, navigating the cars and big rigs for cover like she'd been born to do it.

And then...headlights down the decline. The sedan flying off the highway.

And Lily speeding up again, putting distance between us and the tail.

Two minutes. Maybe three had passed. Max.

But inside my heart, my mind, it was like two millennia had gone by.

"Damn," Lily said, grinning as she zipped up the highway, navigating an interchange and getting onto another freeway that I knew she'd memorized. Because she was always prepared. Because she'd spent her time in the passenger seat, not consuming ketchup like I had, but reviewing the paper maps we'd picked up. Because she was fucking good at her job. Because she had a big heart and total BAMFness and...

Because she made me *feel*.

Fuck. I was just pretending with all the concrete, wasn't I?

Pretending that I'd patched over the holes Lily had made in my walls. Because she'd always been in.

Always.

Even when I pretended otherwise.

My heart thudded. Apparently, it just took a car chase and copious amounts of ketchup to get me to realize…

I wanted Lily.

So much.

Even though part of me thought I didn't deserve her. Even though I was worried I would suck her into the quicksand of my life.

Even though—

No.

She was right before. I was punishing myself, and I was fucking tired of it, tired of wanting and having nothing. Tired of pain and bloody nails and being alone.

Because Lily didn't make me feel alone.

"That made me hungry," she finished as I was processing all that I was feeling within my concrete enclosure—pride and approval, need and certainty, respect for her abilities, and…more.

It was terrifying.

Because it was something that I'd never allowed myself to consider.

Something, I realized with a dawning sense of horror and, if I really studied it (which I wasn't going to at that moment because my head was spinning enough for the time being) that had nothing to do with punishment and everything—*everything* —to do with living.

Living big and free.

Living…

With something—*someone*—that might be a reward.

The best fucking reward of my life.

And maybe, maybe I could be hers, too.

If I tried hard enough.

I was soaking in all that when Lily reached for the bag at my feet and declared, "You better have saved me some fries."

Car chases.

Maps memorized.

French fries.

All the feels.

But...I hadn't saved her any fries.

Fuck.

CHAPTER ELEVEN

LILY

I DROVE for longer than my original shift.

Much longer, not wanting to stop until we put some distance between the tail and ourselves, defaulting to our backup route, long enough to make sure we showed up on a few highway cameras.

Then ditching the car, backtracking, and heading south again.

My eyes were burning by the time I pulled into the gas station to refuel—Kenny tucked into the back of the hatchback, covered with blankets so we looked like a party of three instead of four, my hair tucked under a hat, my frame covered in bulky clothes, a nose prosthesis attached to my face, contacts changing the color of my eyes, Linc and Hannah similarly adorned, though the former was now spotting a beard and a fake belly, and Hannah had changed into a pair of heels (with a stiletto, literally, in each stiletto heel) and a clinging dress.

I hit the bathroom, grabbed a sandwich, chips, a drink, some candy that was terrible for me, but I knew would taste good, especially since I'd subsisted most of the day on a cold hamburger and a few fry dredges (and let me just say that European hamburgers were not as good as their American counterparts).

I checked out with cash, making certain to keep my face averted from the surveillance cameras.

No need to create a digital trail.

I slipped out the front door, moved into the back seat, and started to down my food.

A few minutes later, Hannah hit the driver's seat, Linc the front passenger's, and we were off, zipping away from the city proper, winding through some seriously dark and occasionally twisting roads.

Which was probably why Hannah didn't see it.

Why none of us did.

I was focused on my treats, on the sleep that would soon be forthcoming.

The rest of the car was subdued, focused on the task at hand.

We went around a curve, and—

Crash.

My head whipped forward, and I promptly choked on the bite of candy bar I'd taken, coughing as the seat belt tightened and my body lurched forward. Luckily, the abrupt locking of the belt to stop my forward momentum meant that the chunk of candy flew out of my throat.

That was the last lucky thing that happened, though.

Because then the car flipped.

It was quiet.

Almost silent—my pulse thumping in my ears, my coughing from the near-choking the only things I heard.

We went airborne and the universe seemed to hold…for one long moment.

Then it was *loud,* ear-piercingly loud as the car collided with the asphalt, glass shattering, metal screeching, the vehicle sliding, *sliding* until it hit the embankment at an angle, jarring to a stop.

And then…it was quiet again.

I sucked in a breath, trying to ignore the blood rushing to my head—seeing as I was hanging upside down—and inched my fingers toward my knife. "Hannah?" I whispered. "Linc?"

Nothing.

Movement at my back, the glint of a knife blade held in a bloody hand.

A bloody, splint-covered hand.

I flinched, trying to dodge. But I didn't move fast enough.

The blade sliced toward me—

Fuck. *Fuck!*

It sank into…

The seat, less than an inch from my thigh, far too close to my still-healing wound for comfort. But it wasn't my leg, and then I was moving—falling ungracefully, really—collapsing to the roof of the car, glass digging into my palms.

"Here," Kenny said, and I pushed myself up enough to see that he was on the roof, too, our bags scattered all around him. "Here," he said again, holding out the knife we'd taken off him in the alley. I reached for it, intending to use it to free Linc and Hannah, but Kenny grabbed my wrist, the fiberglass of his splint digging into my skin. "No," he added hurriedly, taking the shaft and twisting it to reveal a hidden compartment inside. "Take it," he whispered. "Take it and use it. If I—" A shake of his head. "If I don't make it out of here, if I *do*, take it and use it to keep Amy safe."

I was frowning when he slapped the shaft of the knife against my palm, a USB drive falling out. He closed my fingers around it.

"Keep her safe."

I nodded, tucking the USB away for safekeeping, closing the shaft, so the hidden compartment was concealed once more. Kenny moved searching through the bags, hopefully to find something useful that we could use to get us the fuck out of here.

I voted for a teleportation device.

Or an air rescue.

Or barring either of those, some firepower that would give us a fighting chance since clearly this route was fucked.

Hannah groaned from the driver's seat.

"Fuck me," she muttered, and I relaxed marginally. We still needed to assess the situation and get the fuck out of this car, but Hannah cussed as easily as she breathed, so if she was cussing, she was breathing.

And she was all right.

Which meant I was breathing easier.

I spun, holding the knife tight. "Brace yourself," I ordered.

Her gaze hit mine, and though she had blood dripping down her temple and that tight dress of hers had a serious wardrobe malfunction happening, she gripped the steering wheel. "Go."

I cut.

She was free, grunting when her body hit the roof of the car, and turned to reach for Linc's seat belt—

And that was when gunshots rang out.

"Fuck," I hissed, moving toward Linc, who was still out, though he was stirring, head moving from side to side, hands opening and clenching.

"Move your ass," Kenny ordered, returning fire, his gun discharging as bullets hit the exterior of the car, as they ricocheted through the windows, flying through the space around us. "I've got one of the Glocks to use for cover, and that's it." We needed Linc free. We needed out of this metal box that was providing as much coverage as Swiss Cheese. And we needed it now.

"Got him," Hannah muttered, gripping Linc's shoulders.

I cut the belt.

Hannah heaved, I heaved, and then the three of us were in

the back seat...or rather, since the car had flipped, two of us were crouched on the roof above the back seat, one—Linc—was sprawled. Linc groaned and his eyes peeled open. "Fucking hell, that's going to leave a mark," he muttered, shifting so that he was up next to us, shaking his head and immediately reaching for his ankle holster and pulling out his gun. Hannah had yanked off the heels from her stilettos, removed the narrow blades hidden within.

I had the USB, the knife. Hannah the blades. Linc one gun and maybe a spare magazine if we were lucky.

And Kenny was running out of bullets.

Fucking hell.

On that thought, the gunfire cut out.

The world fell quiet.

And I knew we had to move.

Rearing back, I kicked out the remnants of the glass, glanced from side to side and shimmied out. "Come on," I hissed, scanning our surroundings, searching for cover as Hannah slipped out behind me, paused to yank up her dress. It was bullet and knife resistant, same as mine was, but considering the amount of bullets that had been flying through the air not too long before, I wouldn't be opposed to her having a bit more fabric covering the pertinent parts.

There was a car stopped behind us on the curve of the shoulder, empty and lights off.

There was a drop-off to our left.

Trees in the distance to our right.

And in front of us, on the other side of the car, a van, headlights on, several people standing outside it, weapons hanging at their sides.

Waiting.

For what?

We stayed crouched, covering Linc as much as possible with blades as he slid out the window.

"Trees?" he asked.

Hannah nodded. "We need cover, and we need it now. They're not going to wait long, and Rochester isn't going to make it far."

"We should split up—" Linc began.

"*No.*" A hiss. "We stick together."

She bent, started to reach into the car, but Kenny was already crawling out, the weapons bag in his hand that he threw at our feet.

"Let's not give them time to get their shit together," he snapped. "We need to *move.*" Linc started to reach for him, but Kenny got to his feet, crouching so the car was blocking his frame. "Now."

"Hannah," Linc began again. "Maybe we should break into two groups—"

"We're not splitting up."

Followed by sharp words from Kenny. "We don't. We die."

"I—" Hannah cut herself off and then her gaze flicked away from us, down the road, and mine followed, understanding now why the bullets had stopped, why those on the other side of the car were waiting. "Fuck," she whispered.

They were watching and waiting because—

"Call it," Kenny snapped. "Let's move."

Orders from a former team leader.

Ones that might normally make another leader bristle or get into a pissing contest.

But Hannah was smarter than that.

She didn't like it. I knew her well enough to see that clearly, but I also knew her frustration was because of the situation, because everything had gone FUBAR, and less to do with Kenny deeming to give orders.

Though, I knew she'd make it clear later that she didn't like that either.

"Too fucking far to run," she muttered, bending toward the bag and unzipping it. "Too much fucking open space." She began gathering together pieces of a rifle, which she tossed to

Linc, then reached back inside and pulled out a canister that would lay down some smoke, pulled the tab and rolled it behind us.

In the direction we both had been looking just seconds before.

"Gotta fucking do shit I don't want to." A sigh. Then her eyes came to mine. "You get your ass to that car parked at the curb. We draw them away. You get it started. We rendezvous back at the highway."

"Han—"

I didn't like the idea of them playing mouse to the fucking cats who far overpowered us. But I also could hear sirens in the distance, knew that if we executed this right, then we had a chance.

A flash of her eyes. "Car. Highway."

I swallowed hard and nodded. "Car. Highway."

"On three," she said, holding up another canister, finger looped through the pin. She pulled the pin, rolled the can under the car. We tensed, waiting as the smoke began pouring out, filling the air, joining the cloud behind us that had finally gotten big enough to fill the night air.

To provide a little bit of cover.

A curse across the street.

The smoke getting thicker.

And...bullets. Flying through the air again, forcing us to duck down.

And...three more vans pulling up behind us.

What Hannah and I had seen. What they must have been waiting for.

"Fuck," Linc whispered.

Hannah tossed the final canister as those bullets flew, cover for me to make it to the car. "One. Two. Three. *Move!*" she ordered.

And...we *moved*.

Hauling ass for the tree line, for the cover there, to draw

them away from the vehicles. The rest of the team continued into them as I peeled off from the other three, and using the cloud of smoke as cover, hit the asphalt, rolled, and slid beneath the car.

Then I went still.

Slowed my breathing.

And waited for the smoke to clear, the bullets to stop flying.

And as they did…

I held my breath.

Because footsteps approached the car, the spot where I was hiding.

Slow. Steady. *Quiet* breathing.

A flashlight beam hit the rear tire, skated up…and then it drifted underneath.

Illuminating my hiding place.

CHAPTER TWELVE

Hannah

I SHOULD HAVE STAYED with her.

I should have stuck with my instinct to not split up.

But they'd stopped shooting and those vans had been coming, and I knew, *I knew* that her having a vehicle gave her the best chance of survival.

If they took us down as we ran—and Rochester lumbered—through the woods, then at least Lily would be safe.

But now we'd slipped free, were waiting at the rendezvous point.

And Lily should have been here.

She wasn't.

It was getting late, the sun would be up soon, and we had to move.

I knew it.

Linc knew it.

Rochester—given the huffing and sighing—*really* fucking knew it.

Considering I'd practically had to haul his ass through the

forest while covering our tracks, this didn't make me happy. It *definitely* didn't make me happy when Linc had veered off to lay a diversion and tracks in a different direction before circling back up to meet with us. And I certainly wasn't happy to be hauling Rochester's ass all while having to avoid the cops who'd apparently decided to get their asses in gear and join in on the search for us.

No doubt the Confederate had gotten to them, too, considering their slow response to an explosion and a hail of gunfire. Yeah, we were on the edge of the city, but explosions and hails of gunfire usually drew police like flies to honey.

Not moseying their way to the scene of the crime.

Then joining forces with the bastards trying to get to Rochester and the information he had, the information he'd provided—namely by eliminating us all.

We'd gone off-grid on this transport.

Laila, Skye, and Jeff would know something was wrong when we missed our scheduled check-in, and they'd probably be able to deduce exactly what had gotten fucked—if the explosion and gunfire made the news.

Which it probably wouldn't.

Because if the Confederate had gotten to the police, then they had probably gotten to the media.

The service providers.

A few keystrokes and the internet went off.

A phone call and no stories were published.

Rochester shifted on his feet. Probably because he was hurting with those healing bones and wounds. Not that I gave a fuck. "We—"

I spun, grabbed the front of his shirt. "I know," I growled. "I fucking *know*, but I'm giving her five more minutes, so shut the fuck about—"

An engine in the distance.

Headlights coming around the corner.

We crouched, studied the approaching car, my heart sinking when I saw it wasn't the one from the sight of the explosion.

It slid to a stop.

I braced, fingers tightening on the blades I'd pulled out of my shoes…this being after righting this fucking dress again. Because as soon as Lily got here, my first piece of business was to get a fucking dress that didn't have either my tits or pussy hanging out.

And seriously, I didn't care if I drew the short straw. I was never wearing something like this again.

The car idled for a moment, and I held my breath, sweat prickling on my nape, adrenaline beginning to pump through my veins as I waited for gunfire to ring out or rocket launchers to appear or the world to explode again.

Whir.

The window rolled down. "You bitches gonna get in?"

I'D DUMPED THE DRESS. Or rather, I'd added jeans and a hoodie, so I had a bullet and knife-resistant tube top that protected my important parts.

No more wardrobe malfunctions.

And no more Rochester.

We'd dumped his ass in Greece, locked down the safe house, and then used a boat for some private transit to Italy. From there, another boat, several trains, and one car later, we'd arrived in France.

Laila and company were still working on their target. Skye and her team had sent him to lockup with a twenty-four-hour guard, giving him some time to think about his future (sit and stew and fingers crossed, he'd break). The hope was that he wouldn't get taken out before they got something good out of him.

But, at this point, I didn't give a fuck.

Because we were spinning again, running in circles.

Jeff and his team had been pulled off this. They'd had a mission get hot for another case, so they'd peeled away to take care of that.

So, it was just us off the southern coast of France, in a location that was so romantic and so much the antithesis of what we'd been dealing with the last week that it was almost funny.

The house we were in was located on the cliffside, a sharp drop to the ocean below. A clear flat swathe of land on all sides, easier to keep watch.

And Linc, Jesse, Leo, Lily, and I were regrouping.

Looking into a church Lily had discovered that appeared suspicious, doing a deep dive on the owners, trying to track any data—basically the boring as fuck part of being a KTS agent. Not every moment could be gunfights and car chases, explosions and delivering targets to safe houses.

"And then there's this," Lily said after we'd all set up our equipment and started breaking up the necessary items to research.

Leo was on first watch.

The rest of us would work.

I glanced from my laptop across the table to Lily, where she was holding up a USB drive. "Kenny gave it to me in the car."

"What is it?" I asked.

"I don't know. He just gave it to me and told me to use it to keep Amy safe."

"Is there a reason you're just bringing it to our attention now?" I asked archly.

"Other than the fact that Kenny gave it to me two seconds before bullets began flying, we split up after a bunch of other baddies came to back up the baddies that fucking flipped our vehicle in the first place. Oh, or maybe there was the slight detail that the car you ordered me to hotwire didn't have an *engine* in it, so I had to hoof it through the forest five miles to find one, all while avoiding the police and bad guys, including the one who shone a flashlight under the flipping car I was hiding beneath so I had to freaking roll and dodge like I was playing Twister in about six inches of space, all *before* the hoofing it."

She swept her hair up into a ponytail, and my gaze was drawn to the slender column of her throat, and as she kept talking, I had a hard time focusing on the words, on the sass she was spouting, the sass that made her sexy as hell, and the sass that reminded me of the revelation I'd had in the car, way back before gunfire and cars flipping and long fucking drives to drop a traitor off in a safe house—a *traitor!*

I knew it was for the greater good.

Rochester had given us some good information, and apparently also a USB with the rest of it.

"Oh, *or maybe*," she sassed on, "I should have told you when we were driving for eighteen hours straight and trying to stay off cameras, undetected at border crossings, and then sneaking him into the safe house with his tiny, adorable daughter who loves all things makeup. Or *maybe* I should have told you on the boat ride where someone might have overheard. Or—"

"Or maybe," Linc muttered, tapping at his keyboard, "you can stop with the *or maybes* and tell us what's on the drive?"

She wrinkled her nose, a hint of pink on her cheeks. "Well, I don't *know* what's on it."

Linc raised a brow. "Because of the aforementioned *or maybes*."

"No." That nose wrinkled further. "Okay. Fine. Yes. Though, I'd also add the *or maybe* because of the car ride and securing the house, along with incognito stops for food, gas, and toilets."

Fuck, she was cute.

Fuck, I liked her.

Fuck, I *wanted* her.

Light and cute. A bright spot in my dark life. Everything I should allow myself to have and everything I knew was inevitable that I *would* have. Because from the moment I'd kissed her, the moment I'd pushed her away, I'd been slipping down this slope.

No, from the moment I'd first fought to get her on my team, the moment I'd allowed myself to be friends, to get that glimpse of her...

It was inevitable.

I was going to fall for her.

I *had* fallen for her.

I was broken inside, full of jagged edges and hidden pits, spikes protruding from the shadows. I should continue what I'd been doing for years—keeping my distance, covering up those pits, dulling the edges and spikes.

I just...couldn't.

I knew in the car, staring at her glowing from the excitement of the car chase. I knew it when my stomach churned as I'd waited for her to show up after we'd split up.

I'd known it...years ago.

Because I wanted Lily to wield the file to soften the sharp, the hammer and nails to build over the holes.

It was selfish. I was bad for her.

But...I couldn't let her go.

So, I was going to take her, make her mine, *and* together we would take down the Confederate.

CHAPTER THIRTEEN

L<small>ILY</small>

THE *CLICK* of the door opening had me jumping.

Mostly because I was naked except for a towel, the shower running in the background, steam filling the air.

I'd passed the USB off to Linc after having no luck processing the data on it.

Probably because I'd hoofed it through the woods for five miles, hotwired a car, picked up my team, and then spent the next forty-eight hours getting Kenny reunited with his daughter and setting up a new home base off KTS's grid.

We didn't know how far the taint went, so staying off official channels was critical.

Burner phones for our teams, including Skye's, Jeff's, and Laila's. Fresh laptops bought with cash that Jesse and Leo had grabbed from a hidey-hole. Encrypted internet, firewalls, VPNs.

We'd pulled out all the security stops, stayed as invisible as possible.

And we all knew that it would still only be a matter of time before the Confederate found us. We just…needed to find more information about them, enough to shift a few more pieces.

We just needed that piece to break this all open.

Hopefully, the USB would bring that.

And hopefully my deep dive into the church would pan out.

Because my gut said it might be the key to everything.

I turned when the door shut, saw Hannah leaning back against it, arms crossed, eyes hot on mine. No. Not *hot*. She'd made it crystal fucking clear that she didn't want me, that we wouldn't ever be what I wanted.

Which bore the question of why she was in the bathroom while I was wearing nothing but a towel.

It was supposed to be my turn to clean up, to sleep.

Hannah wasn't on till third watch.

"What's the matter?" I asked.

She tilted her head to the side, hazel eyes sparking. "You're beautiful, you know that, right?"

I inhaled sharply. "What are you doing?"

She took a step forward, another, and my breath stuttered. Then she was in front of me, the toes of her boots nearly touching my bare ones. "Never in my life have I seen a woman more beautiful." Her eyes dropped, and her gaze was like a physical caress—along my jaw, down my throat, lower to where the towel was wrapped around my breasts, to the bottom edge of it, my bared thighs, calves, toes with chipped pink nail polish.

"Hannah," I whispered.

One finger grazed over my collarbone. "You know I'm fucked up inside."

"*Hannah*," I whispered a little louder.

"You know what they did to me, what the church did, how I felt when they all disowned me."

I *did* know.

She'd told me during one drunken night. Our team had pulled off a mission that seemed like it was going to be fucked, and somehow, *somehow*, it had all straightened out, gone as smoothly as a baby's bottom, and we'd celebrated.

Then everyone else had gone to bed, and Hannah and I had celebrated some more.

Eventually we'd gotten sloppy and started sharing. Funny shit. Stupid shit. Shit our parents did—namely that my parents were great but crazy—going so far as to decorate their Christmas tree in rainbow colors the year I came out (junior year in college) and we went on a vacation the following spring that they called my gaycation so I could explore myself (awkward, obviously, with my parents in tow, but still one of my favorite trips ever because I'd gotten to spend that time with my mom and dad and they had been so excited to be wing-people for me it had been impossible to not get swept up in the moment). But truly, that was the least of their crazy. The first time—no, *my* first time—they'd come into my bedroom, snapped a picture of my girlfriend and me cuddling (and thankfully beneath the covers) then had given me a bouquet of balloons.

A bouquet.

Of balloons.

I loved them, but they were insane…and I still had the picture.

It should be in the dictionary under awkward.

I loved it anyway.

Because I loved them and they loved me, and I was so fucking lucky to have them.

But then because I'd shared and because I was beyond drunk and had absolutely no filter, I'd asked Hannah about *her* first time, and her face had gotten sad, and I'd regretted it immediately.

She'd shared about her parents being assholes—namely because they'd disowned her after she'd struggled for years about what she was feeling because their church was strict and didn't approve of it and she knew and tried to fight it…

But there was no fighting it.

Hannah was who she was, and that was a beautiful person. She worked her ass off, risked her life for innocent people, had a big, kind heart that, yes, she protected heavily, but once a person was in within those fortified walls, they knew that they would have Hannah.

Her protection. Her strength. Her big, kind heart.

Maybe it was hard for some to see.

But it hadn't been hard for me.

It was why I loved her…and why I loved her enough to not step over the barrier she'd erected between us.

Her finger drifted over my skin again, drawing me out of my mind, and making me remember that I was in my towel and naked beneath that towel, and Hannah was touching me.

"What's the matter?" I asked again.

"I can't stop thinking about you." Her hand drifted up, cupped my cheek. "About this beautiful face." It slid down, nudged the towel out of the way, and she rested her palm on my chest, just over my heart.

Which was pounding, lurching against my rib cage.

"And this is beautiful, too."

My breathing stuttered, lungs straining. "What are you doing, Hannah?"

"I'm done."

I blinked.

"Fought it for years."

"Fought what?"

"You."

My lips parted, a shuddering breath sliding through. "I—"

"I'm fucked up, but I've tasted you now. I'm fucked up, but I can't keep fighting it. I'm fucked up—"

The shock wore off at the second *I'm fucked up*.

Which was when my temper spiked.

"Shut up," I snapped, gripping her shoulders.

Her brows dragged together.

"Shut. Up," I said again, nails digging in. "You are *not* fucked up. You are *not*," I added when she opened her mouth to argue. "Do you have walls up? Fuck yes. Have you been hurt and that explains why you built those walls? Definitely."

Her hands came up, dislodging mine, lacing our fingers together. "It's not walls, Lil."

I opened my mouth, prepared to argue, but she beat me to it.

"It's concrete, and my nails, my hands are bloody from trying to make it thicker."

I inhaled.

She went on. "Thick-ass concrete I spent my life putting up. Concrete you've been chipping away at, and I been desperately throwing up."

My throat worked hard, guilt swirling. I was in love with Hannah. She was my best friend and an awesome person— smart, sexy, total badass. Because I liked her so much, I didn't like the idea of her panic-smoothing proverbial concrete to keep her walls in place just because I had told her how I felt, because we'd kissed. "I didn't mean to push. You said it couldn't happen, and I backed off."

She lifted my hand, kissed the back of it. "I know you didn't." Her smile flowed against my skin. "And I know you *did*."

"I—"

"You're nice, Lil," she whispered, turning my hand over in her grip, dragging her lips up my wrist. "Too fucking nice for me."

"Hannah—"

"But I'm done with worrying about you being too nice for me. I'm done worrying about me being too fucked up for—"

"Stop saying you're fucked up," I gritted.

She tugged, drawing me forward, bringing her lips to my elbow. "Okay, baby."

"And maybe tell me why you're in here?"

Amusement in her hazel eyes when they came to mine.

"You're in a towel, steam's in the air, my lips are on your skin...
Why do you think I'm here?"

Oh.

Oh.

"But you didn't like it when I kissed you," I blurted.

Lips curving up. "Is *that* what you think?"

I didn't know what the fuck I was thinking.

"Newsflash, baby," she murmured, the words puffing against my skin. "I liked it too much."

I didn't know what I was thinking, but I was still me. And I might be a nice person, but I was still full of snark and sass and spine. Which was why I lifted my chin and asked, "I guess I should have clued into that when your tongue was in my mouth, huh?"

A nip to my jaw. "Yeah, babe, you should have."

"Still doesn't tell me why you're here," I said, and yeah, my voice was breathy, mostly because she'd stepped even closer and her hands were sliding up my back, dipping into my hair, tugging out the tie.

"Yeah, it does," she whispered against my skin, her mouth doing some trailing of its own, lips dragging along my jaw, tongue darting out to taste the skin behind my ear.

I shivered, whispered. "You want me?"

Her fingers tensed in my hair. "I think I'm making that clear."

"All of a sudden," I asked, knowing this was important, that I needed to understand, "your history doesn't matter?"

It killed the moment, a tenseness drifting into the bathroom, tangling with the steam in the air. Hannah lifted her head, her hazel eyes blazing as they hit mine.

"I didn't mean it like that," I whispered. "It's just...nothing's changed except we've spent the last week working our asses off, getting shot at, and going on tilt-a-whirls in cars, and trying to set up safe houses." I shrugged, felt the towel teeter precari-ously. "So really, just a normal week as a KTS agent." My lips tipped up. "Minus the whole trying to save the world from an organization called the Confederate which has fucked-up ties around the globe and in governments and—"

"I don't want to talk about the Confederate," Hannah murmured. "Or my past that"—she cupped my cheek—"isn't going to change."

I frowned. "I don't understand."

A smile. "I know." A beat. "But I'm going to make it so you do."

Apprehension slid through me, and I knew that I'd dreamed of this moment, had pictured Hannah looking at me like this a dozen, a thousand times. But suddenly there. Suddenly *in* the moment it was happening...and I had to admit that panic was slithering through me. "What about the whole, subordinate-boss thing?" I blurted.

She lifted a brow. "What do you mean?"

I cleared my throat, eyes going to one of the hooks on the wall, seeing that it hung crooked when compared to the others. "I mean, technically you're my boss."

"*That's* what you're worried about during this particular juncture in time?"

"Well, I'm not worried about the moon landing, for fuck's sake."

Laughter in her eyes, and fuck if that didn't make Hannah look like the most beautiful woman I'd ever seen. "You're worried about being in a relationship with me when you're my second in command?"

I narrowed my eyes. "Well, yes. It's an HR nightmare."

More laughter, this time out loud, and the sound was sunlight on a cool winter morning, kissing my cheekbones, alighting on my lips. Then I actually listened to the words coming out of her mouth.

And wanted to punch her.

"You're worried about us dating each other when people are fucking and dating and getting hitched, and then doing it all over again at KTS more often than the characters on *Gray's Anatomy?*"

She had a point.

She was still an asshole.

Which I told her.

"You're an asshole."

Her lips just twitched, and she traced her fingers around the shell of my ear. "We'll get Linc involved. He's fair to a fault and neutral."

"Not true," I said pertly, lifting my chin. "He likes me better."

A grin, but she kept going. "We deal with orders like we always have. When I put out there something you don't like, you talk and I listen. I make a decision, make changes if I think that's the right thing to do. We do it. You still don't agree, Linc's the intermediary. He makes the final call."

"Just that easy?"

She shrugged. "Yup." Her eyes went suddenly serious. "Minus one thing. If it's life or death or needs to happen quickly, you do what we've always done. Head down, listen up, and get through. Debrief later."

That *was* what we did.

And it worked.

Because shit got hot sometimes, and we didn't always have time to sit down and hash it out. Not until later anyway.

"Okay," I whispered.

"Okay?" she repeated.

"On one condition," I said.

More brow-lifting. "If I think it's too dangerous, you'll pause, consider, and listen, no matter how intense things are getting."

No hesitation. "Okay."

"Just like that?"

Her fingers drifted down my throat. "Just like that."

"So wh-what else *are* we going to talk about?" I asked, pulse speeding, desire coiling in my middle.

Her brows lifted, a smirk teasing her lips. "Wasn't really planning on talking."

Heat curled through my stomach; moisture began to gather between my legs. I *could* pretend it was from the shower running, but it wasn't. It was all Hannah and her hot eyes and her body close to mine.

"I just..."

She smoothed back a tendril of hair that was curling in the humidity of the space. "You just *what?*"

"I'm not a have sex on the first date kind of girl."

Warmth drifting into her eyes, fingers smoothing my hair. "I know, baby."

"And..."

"What?"

"And I still don't understand how a little more than a week ago you were pushing me away, and today you're invading my shower, telling me you want me and—"

"Ketchup."

I blinked. "Ketchup?"

"I sat in the front seat on the drive, before our plan went to shit, and we were scrambling. I spent my time in the passenger's seat, stuffing my face with fries, well, with mostly ketchup."

My brows drew together, but my lips twitched.

"And you," she said gently. "You spent your time in that seat reviewing maps you'd picked up in the gas station instead of cramming food down your throat. You spent your time thinking about everyone else instead of yourself." Fingers along my jaw, my bottom lip. "*You* spend your time working so hard, killing yourself for everyone else, for your teammates, for people you'll never even meet, and the one time you wanted more, wanted something for yourself, and for some fucking reason wanted *me*, I denied you that."

She sucked in and released a breath, fingers drifting down until her hand cupped the side of my neck. "And…you said I might deserve the punishment because I was too stuck punishing myself to live, to love."

Fuck. That sliced through me.

So much guilt. So many careless words.

"I'm sorry," I said, "I didn't mean—"

"You were right." The blunt rejoinder snapped me into silence.

I blinked at her.

"And I *am* tired of it."

Quiet for a long beat before I asked cautiously, "So you're going to stop punishing yourself and your plan to do that is by being with me?"

A shrug. A smile. "Yup."

"Because of ketchup?" I asked.

Another shrug, her smile growing wider. "Yup."

"Okay, I'm confused," I admitted out loud, not that she wouldn't have been able to pick up on that in my words. I was also a little scared and turned on and…felt like I was holding my breath, waiting for the next big thing.

"That's fine. Because I'll make it clear to you in time."

Whoosh.

My stomach took a ride on a roller coaster.

"You will?"

"Yup."

That didn't give me much. Hell, if I were being honest, it didn't give me anything. "Um…"

"Right after I kiss you."

Whoosh again.

"I—"

Her lips dropped to mine.

CHAPTER FOURTEEN

Hannah

SOFT.

Her lips were like damp clouds, and part of my brain was processing that ridiculous metaphor when those lips parted, and I dipped my tongue in to taste.

Then *her* tongue moved, sliding against mine, and she moaned softly.

Barely audible.

But I heard it, and it sent heat arrowing down between my legs, had my fingers itching to tug the towel off and dip between hers.

My breasts grew heavy, nipples brushing the inside of my bra.

From a kiss.

From *her* kiss.

Her arms tightened around me, bringing her body flush to mine, and she breathed my name, saying it softly against my lips before she turned her head, dragged her lips over my jaw, dipping it lower.

Then her mouth came back to mine, and her moan was louder this time, skating down my spine and filling me with heat. I ached. I needed. I *wanted.*

I plunged my hands into her hair, deepening the kiss, running my tongue over hers, hauling her closer. She gripped my shoulders and I turned, lifting her onto the vanity, stepping between her thighs. The towel had rucked up so when we broke apart. to suck in air, my gaze drifted down, and I saw...

Strong, bare thighs, spread wide.

A shadow of damp heat.

"Fuck," I whispered, releasing her, stepping back, and straightening the towel as I went.

"Hannah?" she asked, her eyes glazed when the lids slowly peeled open.

Glazed from a kiss.

Glazed from *my* kiss.

Fuck again.

That glaze began to fade, probably because I was standing there like an idiot, my chest heaving, my hands clenched.

"What's the matter?" she whispered.

A breath blown out; control regained. I stepped toward her, cupping her cheek. "Take your shower, baby."

Not a first date girl.

Fuck, we hadn't even *had* a date.

Two kisses. Years of friendship.

But the touching, *new*. The kissing, *new*—and the last time it had ended with me shoving her away. Me saying I wanted her after keeping all that distance? Newsflash...it was also new. Plus, Lily just had a towel on, and I didn't have enough clothes on myself to stop this from getting out of hand if she kept kissing me the way she had been (which, true story, would probably require me wearing a suit of armor to stop those kisses from one or both of us getting naked). Add in me wanting her for so long, especially after having denied to myself for so long....and anyway, I wasn't exactly feeling the most confident in adhering to the boundaries she'd set up.

I swallowed hard, stepped back again, moved toward the door, fingers grasping the knob.

"Han—"

"Shower and sleep, baby." I grasped the knob, turned it.

"You're going to leave me like this?" she asked, eyes going wide.

There was so much moisture in the air that tiny droplets had formed on her hair, on her skin, were dripping down between her breasts, making me fucking pissed at the towel.

I wanted to will it out of existence.

Which made my mouth water, tongue desperate to catch those droplets.

"What?" I whispered.

"You're going to leave me like *this*?" she repeated.

"Like what?"

A heated gaze measuring mine. Mischief on the edge of chocolate eyes. And I knew, *knew* I was so totally fucked.

Knew it when I got a husky response. "Wet and aching and desperate for you."

I cleared my throat, thought about the one thing guaranteed to temper my libido.

Penises.

For once, it didn't work, especially when her legs parted, and the towel rucked up and—

I tried logic. "You said you weren't a first date girl."

A sexy curve of those lips I'd just tasted, those lips I wanted with every part of me to taste again. "I wasn't aware that you cornering me in the bathroom was a first date."

Surprise weaving through me.

Heat arrowing straight to my pussy.

I pushed away from the door. "I—"

"So, technically, this *isn't* a first date." Lily slid off the vanity. "Which means we can ignore my rules." She smiled wider as she reached for the towel, tugged it open, and dropped it to the floor.

I'd seen her naked before, but in that locker room way, eyes catching a nipple, a flash of curls, and diverting my gaze.

This.

This.

Was all Lily, from head to toe and I could look as long as I wanted.

Pink-painted toes, strong legs. All that was left of her earlier wounds was a small bandage on her thigh, a waterproof wrap on her wrist. My eyes tracked those, a blip of rage at Rochester all over again. But I banked that anger because it was Lily in front of me, Lily who had dropped the towel, Lily who was standing there naked and vulnerable and beautiful, but because I was frozen like a statue of an idiot, a glimmer of insecurity was entering her gorgeous brown eyes.

"You're beautiful," I said, moving toward her, dropping my hands to her hips, sliding them up her torso, stopping just shy of her breasts.

"You said that already."

I grinned at the sass. "I believe I said you were the most beautiful woman I've ever seen." A beat. "And it's true."

"Then why are you standing there barely touching me when I gave you the green light?"

This woman. So much talking, so little doing.

But I supposed that was my fault. I was the one who was standing there, not touching any of the good parts, and she was naked, all but asking me to fuck her. "You confused with me the no sex on the first date thing, Lil."

"Well," she murmured, rising on tiptoe, "get *un*confused."

"Baby?"

"Yeah?"

"Shut up."

A flash of humor, her lips parting to say something else, but I'd had enough. I bent and took her lips, kissing her long and deep, until my lungs screamed for air, and even when we broke apart

I nuzzled at her throat, wrapping my arms around her, sliding them down her spine.

And cupping that ass.

A gorgeous, fucking ass that I had been desperate to touch for ages, and now I had my hands on it…and it was glorious. I massaged and cupped, groped and stroked. Her hips canted forward, and I took my time getting my fill. For the moment. Because as good as her ass was, there was a long list of other things that I wanted to touch more. Promising myself I'd worship her ass like it deserved later, I bent and kissed her, letting my hands do some wandering—well, *more* wandering.

Drifting forward over her hips, sliding up over the softness of her abdomen, up further, trailing my fingertips along her sides, her rib cage, feeling goose bumps prickle up on her skin. This time I didn't stop below her breasts, tracing lightly along the bottom curve of one soft globe and then the other, feeling her breath catch in our kiss and breaking it so I could trail my mouth along her throat.

Getting closer to those fucking gorgeous tits.

Freeing her mouth so I could hear her moans, her breath hitching.

Skin like silk. Silk that smelled like flowers. Somehow after the week we'd had her skin still smelled like flowers.

I inhaled deeply and then bent further, lips drifting over her breasts, tasting her there, trailing my tongue over the soft skin, closer and closer to one of the sensitive, hardened nubs.

"Hannah," she whispered when my tongue ghosted over her nipple.

Her hands had come to my head, fingers winding into my hair, holding me there, and I took the silent invitation, bent a little further, and then sucked her nipple into my mouth.

"*Oh*," she moaned, holding me tighter. "That's—yes—honey, keep doing that."

Not gonna stop.

Especially not when her hands dipped down and scooted under my shirt, caressing my skin, slipping under the band of my bra. She squeezed and teased, slowly driving me insane, as she fondled me and played with my nipples, but as much as I liked it, I wanted this to be about her, so I wrapped my arms around her, lifted her up, and set her back on the vanity. Then I stepped close again, and I took my time, kissing and sucking, massaging and stroking her breasts.

Until she was panting and her hands were pulling tightly at my hair.

Until her skin was flushed, and her moans were getting louder.

Until she writhed against me, and I *had* to taste her.

I dropped to my knees, pressed her thighs apart, and moved in close. "Roses," I muttered. "How the fuck do you smell like roses everywhere?"

"Shh," she murmured, arching a little closer.

I nibbled at her thigh. "You do."

"*Shh,*" she muttered, hands back in my hair, tugging me nearer. I went, dragging my tongue up the inside of her leg, moving toward her pussy.

A tentative touch of my tongue, just gauging how sensitive she might be.

At that light caress, she jumped, hissing, legs tightening around me, trying to grind down on my face.

Very sensitive.

Very responsive.

Fuck yes.

So, I got to work.

Licking, sucking, circling her clit with my tongue, pressing a finger inside, and then when she began riding it, sliding in another, fucking her with them, fucking her until she was writhing against me, until her head fell back against the mirror, and she bucked against my mouth.

"That's—" Her legs convulsed. "That's—right *there*. Right—oh, my God. Hannah…just a little more. Yes—"

Fuck, she was hot, skin flushed and wet and pink, pussy dripping, her arousal in my nose, on my tongue. So fucking pretty with her eyes half-mast, her breasts jiggling as she fucked my fingers, fucked my face.

I focused, concentrating my efforts on her *right there*, on exactly where she wanted me to be, on the movements and the caresses, the flicks of my tongue that had her crying out, her pussy clenching, her hips bucking.

And then I slid another finger home, curling it, and—

"Oh fuck," she breathed. "Oh fuck, oh fuck, oh—"

I reached up, rolled one nipple between thumb and fore-finger on this side of shy of too hard, just like she'd liked it, just like it had made her writhe and moan not long before.

And that touch was enough to send her that final distance, to catapult her over the edge, her pussy clenching tightly around my fingers, her clit swelling, all those internal muscles working together as she came, and did it hard.

On my face.

With that rose-scented pleasure in my nose.

With her moans in my ears.

With her hands in my hair, her legs over my shoulders—

With *all* of Lily. On me, wrapped around me, in my heart.

A reward.

My reward.

And I was never letting her go.

It took a long time for her to catch her breath, but the whole time she did so, she ran her fingers through my hair, down my nape, tracing patterns on my skin.

Eventually, she straightened, tugged me out from between her legs, stared deeply into my eyes.

"Ketchup?" she asked.

I grinned. "Ketchup."

CHAPTER FIFTEEN

LILY

I'D TRIED TO RECIPROCATE.

But Hannah had simply made sure I was steady on my feet then insisted I shower before all the hot water in the house ran out.

Then she'd gone.

Now, I'd had a shower (about half of it being hot, considering how long it had been running before I'd actually gotten into it) and I was beyond ready to crash.

I *should* find Hannah and discuss what happened further.

I *should* understand exactly what was happening.

I didn't.

Because I was tired and had been pleasured within an inch of my life and…

She was in my bed.

"Umm…"

She lifted the covers. "Get in."

To which I—super eloquently—replied, "Umm…"

Hannah slid out of the bed, wearing a T-shirt and shorts.

Nothing particularly sexy or revealing, but she was still the sexiest woman I had ever seen. But she didn't give me much time to appreciate the view because her arm went around my waist and then she was ushering me into the bed, pushing me down onto the mattress, and tugging the blankets up and over us.

My pussy clenched, ready for a reenactment of earlier, though, I would be the one fucking Hannah with my tongue, the one giving instead of receiving.

She'd played my body like a goddamned fiddle, discovering the touches that drove me wild and then exploiting them until it had felt like I'd detonated.

Literally—okay, *figuratively*—detonated.

At the very least, I'd had my hardest orgasm ever.

But after she'd tucked the covers around us, her fingers—and mouth—didn't do any walking…or rather, any drifting, stroking, kissing, or licking.

And when my fingers tried to drift down, smoothing over her side and slipping beneath the waistband of her shorts, she captured my hand, laced our fingers together, and drew them up. Pressed a kiss to the back of my hand. Then she wrapped me in her arms, tugged me against her chest, tucking my head beneath her chin.

"What are we doing?" I whispered.

"We're *supposed* to be sleeping," she muttered, running her hand lightly up and down my back.

It was a snapped-out reply.

But one that was so Hannah.

Which meant that I was totally comfortable giving a response that was completely me. "Well, it's kind of hard to reconcile how we're all of a sudden in bed together."

"I told you, it's—"

"Ketchup," I grumbled. "Yeah, yeah. I know. Because *that* makes perfect sense."

Her fingers tangled in my hair. "Should this be the moment I revisit talking about all my fucked-up-ness?"

I scowled but didn't lift up to do it at her.

She knew though, shifting so she could kiss the top of my head. "Stop scowling. Just accept that I've finally gotten it out of my head to stop punishing itself, mostly because of ketchup, but also because you read me the riot act and got me thinking."

I went still—because guilt, so much guilt. "I'm sorry I said those things," I whispered. "It wasn't right. I hurt you and—"

"You did," she said, and the guilt intensified. "But I needed it." Her fingers threaded through my hair again. "You set me straight, baby."

That didn't stop the guilt from coiling tight in my abdomen. "I shouldn't have—"

"I'm *glad* you did. I was punishing myself, and I'll probably do it again at some point because of that fucked-up-ness." I made a sound of protest, but she went on before I could argue that she was perfect (which she wasn't, of course, but I knew she was perfect for me, just like I'd known it six years before when I'd watched her at work and fell head over heels). "Which means," she said. "That I'll need you to go badass on me during all that self-punishment so that you can set me straight again."

I winced.

"If it makes it better," she said lightly, "we can just blame it on the ketchup."

I giggled, slid my arms around her waist. "You realize that I still don't know exactly what we're doing here, don't you?"

A squeeze. "You need me to spell it out for you?" she teased.

"Yeah," I said tartly. "*Please* spell it out for me, O Brilliant Team Leader."

"I want you. You want me. I think you're the most beautiful woman on the planet. You love me." Another squeeze. "So, we're together."

"Just like that?" I asked.

"You want me to send you an engraved invitation?"

My chest shook with laughter. "No."

"So, we're together," she said again.

"And that includes sleeping in the same bed?"

"It includes us spending time together, in a bed, and out of it, at work and not," she said, stroking her hand up and down my back. "It includes us being *together*, and if that being together is as good as I think it will be, it includes being together enough that your mom feels the need to buy you another balloon bouquet."

Now I didn't know whether to laugh or wrap my arms tighter and declare my undying love all over again.

I settled for somewhere in between.

Chuckling and then whispering, "I think Mom would *kill* to buy another balloon bouquet."

"Good, baby," she said softly. "Now sleep."

"I—" I yawned, fighting it because I didn't want to sleep, didn't want to risk waking up and have this not be real, to have this all be some fucked-up dream or fantasy or hallucination. "Should—" Another yawn.

"Talk more tomorrow."

An order.

"We should—"

"*Tomorrow.*" More snapping.

"Hannah—"

One movement had me on my back, her body over mind, her mouth descending. Her lips on mine, her tongue in my mouth. Hannah kissing me until I was limp and wet and—

Then she rolled us again, tucked me against her.

A kiss to the top of my head, her arms wrapped tight.

And even though that kiss turned me on, made me ache and want to reciprocate for earlier all over again, Hannah's warm arms around me, holding me tightly, her even breaths ruffling my hair, had my eyes sliding closed, my body relaxing.

Sleep tugging me under.

———

"COFFEE."

The word was accompanied by a *plunk* and a mug appearing in front of my nose.

I glanced from the steaming mug up to Hannah's face.

And it was a good thing I did that because Hannah was bending down, her face coming down toward mine, her lips not just brushing mine, but kissing me.

Kissing. *Me.*

With tongue and teeth and definitely not appropriate in front of co-workers all huddled together around a large dining room table working intensity.

When she broke away, my heart was pounding, my pussy was…well, not happy (mostly because it wanted her fingers and tongue), and my mind was definitely not on work.

She nipped my ear, murmured, "What? You think I'd hide this? Hide *us?*"

My brows lifted. "No," I whispered. "I just…didn't think that it would involve kissing me senseless when I was trying to work."

Laughter in her eyes, a tug of my ponytail. "Guess you'd better get used to it."

Then she walked away.

Walked away.

Like she hadn't just kissed the shit out of me in front of everyone else.

I gaped and did it for a good long while.

Then I caught a flicker of movement out of the corner of my eye, turned and saw Jesse had her hand extended to Leo.

For a high five.

I glared.

They grinned.

Then Jesse stood and crossed to me, did something she wouldn't have done a year ago—because she'd been too closed off and hurt by her past to truly accept our friendship (and boy was I feeling *that*, along with the fact that it had changed and changed big when she'd found the right person to love her)—and she hugged me and hugged me big and tight while whispering, "About time she got her head out of her ass."

I jerked.

She grinned, squeezed me again.

And how was I supposed to work after all that?

Jesse chuckled. "Talking to yourself out loud is the first sign of love." Another squeeze. "Just saying."

"What?"

"You're wondering how you're supposed to work," Jess said lightly, "but not in your own head like you thought you were."

Oh shit.

"I'm losing it."

"Yeah." Jesse grinned. "But in the best way."

"I have work to do," I whispered.

"Yup."

"We shouldn't be dipping into this now, not with the mission hot and the Confederate out there and—"

"The world is always falling apart, babe. There will always be a crisis, always be a better time." She straightened, walked back to her laptop. "Seize the moment, Lil. Take what you want and live it up."

And seriously, how was I supposed to work with all *that* floating around in my head?

I stared at my screen, and I did it for a while.

Then Leo shuffled some papers. "Just saying"—he shot a grin at Jesse—"you keep fantasizing about your girl and your coffee's gonna get cold."

I jumped, but I did it focusing on my screen, reaching for my cup of coffee.

And thinking Leo wasn't wrong.

The coffee was cold.

But I still drank every last drop.

Because…Hannah had given it to me.

CHAPTER SIXTEEN

Hannah

THREE DAYS LATER, I sat on the cliffside, feet dangling over the edge, leaning back on my hands, and staring at the ocean in the distance.

I'd done my daily shift on watch.

Eaten.

Now I should be heading back inside to take my turn at the computers.

Lily had made some progress on the church, tracking the owners in Berlin through several shell companies and then through several more. Now she was getting close, and I knew this mostly because the pieces of information were coming fewer and farther between.

Getting hot.

Crawling through molasses.

Part because we were being careful. Part because that information was hard to get to.

And Leo, he was getting closer to the USB. He'd broken the

encryption and was making his way through all the information.

The bottom line was money talked.

Rochester had tracked the deposits he'd been given through the Confederate, and through that, he'd done some deep dives into the banks (really, the *trail* of banks that money had been washed through). There were connections there to the mafia and to several drug cartels, but those were players we were all familiar with; those we had on record.

They *weren't* the people who were in the shadows and pulling the strings.

No tattoos. No Latin. No drug dealers or mafiosi infiltrating our bases.

A way to make money.

A way to have enough to work in the shadows.

That had been confirmed. What *hadn't* been was the crossover.

No records of a presence in Atlanta—where a lot of this shit went down. The closest connection was Ava's father—who'd been involved in trafficking and had been head of a branch of the Italian mafia, until KTS had infiltrated, the mission had gone FUBAR, and the Russians had gotten involved.

But that wasn't new information for us.

KTS had been on that mission—Laila's team. We knew it had gotten fucked. We knew we'd lost the mission and nearly lost two agents, Ava and Dan, in the process.

But the USB didn't appear to be the golden ticket Rochester had promised it would be.

Yeah, there was some information on the drive that we hadn't gone through, but it wasn't looking promising. Not like the church connection was.

On that thought, I should get back inside, do my time on the laptops, then shower and get cleaned up...hopefully, with Lily.

Though that was less a hope and more a certainty, considering I'd managed to get her in my bed the last three nights—or in *her* bed, anyway. I hadn't managed a shower *with* her—a fantasy that was now scratched to the top of my Fantasy List, but that would be forthcoming. However, I did manage to get her in my arms every night.

"Hey."

I'd felt her approach, my spine tingling like a built-in Lily Detector.

"Hey," I murmured back, shifting slightly so I could put my arm around her. She had a stack of papers in her hands—because of course she did—and I glanced down, wanting to see what she was working on.

It was a list of names, some crossed out, others unmarked.

And it was what I saw in the un-crossed-out section in that list of names that had me freezing.

I snatched the sheet. "What the fuck?" I brought it closer, literally not able to believe that I was reading what I was reading.

"Han?"

The paper crinkled, my hand drawing into a fist, the page crumpling along with it. "What is this?" I asked, my voice sounding like I'd swallowed gravel.

"A list of names from Kenny's flash drive. Why?"

My brows yanked together, a sick ball of dread curling in my gut. "How many other lists were on there, Lil?"

She frowned. "This was the only one," she murmured, "and so far, I haven't found anything on any of these people."

"Except two," I whispered.

"What?" she asked, still frowning. "Which two?"

I pointed. "*These* two."

She frowned, glanced down to where I was pointing. "Why are they important?"

"Because those two names are my parents."

———

WE WERE SITTING around the table. Even Jesse, who I'd pulled in from perimeter, had joined us.

And we were looking at surveillance footage.

Of my parents.

Arriving in Berlin.

And zoomed in? Black on their hands, the quality of the public camera not good enough to say for certain, but it appeared to be the edges of a tattoo.

Black tattoos on my parents' hands, on the hands of people who were so religious they thought it was a sin for me to color my hair (which I'd done often in high school, making them *very* unhappy, probably the *most* unhappy about…well, before the whole getting caught kissing a girl and getting kicked the fuck out of their house level of unhappiness my actions had garnered).

But for this, they'd marked their skin.

I didn't think it was with a felt tip pen either.

I knew instinctively that they'd done it for something they thought would be for a higher purpose, and, frighteningly, I could easily believe that purpose was for the Confederate.

Because in the hours since I'd seen their names on the list, we'd found *more*.

Because the trail for the money for the church in Berlin dead-ended…at my childhood church.

And when we'd begun vetting the members whose names I remembered, no surprise, they'd all taken trips to Berlin.

But my parents?

They were repeat visitors, and I was guessing that was because they were deacons in the church. Both of them.

And the other four leaders whose names we'd found in sister churches to my childhood congregation, who were also deacons in their church structure?

They had plenty of German stamps in their passports as well.

"Found something else," Leo said, spinning his laptop so we could all see the screen.

A hit on a few of the other names—more churches, six more deacons.

"Keep on the list," I ordered him and turned to Linc. "You stay on my parents." He nodded. "Jess and Lil, let's focus more on surveillance; let's try to get confirmation of the tattoos. I'm going to go on watch, and we'll reconvene if anyone finds anything further."

"This is it," Lily murmured. "I swear, I can feel it and feel it hard."

I felt it, too.

But it was less *hard* and more twisted and sick.

My parents part of the Confederate?

I'd never once considered it.

Never.

But that sick and twisted part of me knew it was the truth. The church had been powerful when I'd been growing up, all but owning the town, and my parents had been all in.

And I mean *all in.*

All in as in daily prayer circles when the sun rose, except for Sundays when the prayer began at sun-up and didn't end until the sun went down. The women in church hadn't been allowed to cut their hair, and definitely no dye. Further that, the men weren't allowed to have long locks either. It was firmly gender roles when it came to hair and clothes, too. As for the women and clothes, there weren't any ankles shown—or, for that matter, shoulders, cleavage, knees, and certainly not any portion of thighs. And for *everyone*, there wasn't any alcohol allowed, nor any drugs. Hell, no music that wasn't hymns was allowed to play in church or home.

My mom played homemaker, followed all those rules, and beat me when I didn't.

And then told my dad.

Who favored the belt as punishment, even after my mom had already given her punishment.

I became intimately acquainted with his belt.

All the way up until I left—was kicked out. *Whatever*. It didn't matter. Not anymore.

"Honey."

I glanced up from the patrol I was doing—and probably doing a shitty job considering I'd barely heard Lily approach, and she wasn't trying to be quiet—and faced Lil.

"Hey," I murmured.

"Come here," she said softly, sinking to the soft grass and patting the spot next to her.

I went, sat down.

She held up a printed page, and I held my breath as she handed it to me.

Then released that breath when I saw the photo.

My parents. Then on the next page, a zoomed-in image, better quality than what we'd been able to get before. On their right hands.

A crescent moon. The set of scales. The inscription.

I knew it would be in Latin, though I couldn't read the squiggles at that moment, and I tried to think back, to wonder if I'd ever seen them with it.

I didn't recall.

But I doubted it.

Because I'd seen those hands rising over me enough times to know that if there had been a tattoo there, I would have seen it. I would have remembered.

So, when had they gotten them?

And why?

Because what the fuck did the Confederate want?

"We've found five more churches," she said softly.

I sucked in a breath. "This is it," I whispered.

"The path to the end," she agreed. "We're going to take these fuckers down."

"Damn right."

"Jesse found a back door into the Congregation of the Sacred Earth."

My parent's church.

"If the information is there, she'll find it."

"She will," Lily agreed. "We all will."

We sat in silence, and I couldn't read minds, so I didn't know what Lily was thinking. Though, if I had to hazard a guess, I would say she was running through additional scenarios to find out more information about the Confederate.

Always working.

Always thinking.

I wanted to spirit her away to some remote island when this was all done, to pry her laptop and cell away from her, and just spend time together.

Just waves and sand and Lily.

Because now that I'd finally allowed myself to have her, I wanted to gorge myself, wanted to use her bright to forget the dark in my past, to chase the shadows away and just live in the now with her.

Considering I'd basically convinced myself that she was thinking of work, driven and focused as always, Lil surprised the shit out of me when she asked, "Are you okay?"

I frowned. "What do you mean?"

"I mean, we just found out that your parents are part of this mysterious group we've been chasing for the last year, and it wasn't like you guys ended things on good terms." She shifted next to me, folding her legs up, resting one across my thigh. "That had to be a shock."

Understatement of the year.

But the history, *my* history wasn't good.

So, it wasn't really a surprise.

What was? That I wanted to give her the rest of it, instead of burying the hurts and old wounds, to expose them to her light and let her reduce them to ash.

The past.

Gone.

Forever.

But to do that, I had to give. "The night I left," I said, "the night they kicked me out, I could barely walk because they beat me so badly, could barely see because my eyes were so swollen." I sucked in a breath, released it slowly. "I would have died if not for Haley."

A long moment of quiet, then, "She was the one you got caught with?"

I nodded. "She...her parents weren't like mine. They weren't happy about it, but they didn't beat her. She got grounded, lost computer privileges. I got"—I sucked in a breath—"six broken ribs and a half-dozen wounds that required stitching."

Her fingers tightened on mine.

"She stole keys to her parents' car, brought me a bag, helped me clean up." I cleared my throat. "Then she drove me to the bus station and bought me a ticket."

"She was one bright spot in that town."

"Yeah," I whispered. "And I left her to that town. To that church."

Lily smoothed her hand over my hair. "We should try to find her."

My brows rose. "You want to track down my ex?"

"I *want* to track down the girl, who is now a woman, who helped *my* woman out of a tight spot, who was left behind in a town that clearly went from really fucked to *absolutely really fucked*."

I hadn't thought about it like that.

"Shit," I whispered.

"I'll track her down," she murmured.

Warmth in my chest, so much warmth that incinerated the cold of the past, that filled me to bursting, that knocked down my walls and made it impossible to not blurt without warning, "Fuck, I love you."

She inhaled sharply. *"Hannah."*

"What?" I asked, dropping my hand to her thigh and squeezing lightly. "You think I don't know what I've got, baby? You think I don't know how fucking incredible you are?"

"Honestly?"

I nodded.

"I'm still recovering from the whirlwind of us going from friends to more. I'm—it's more than I could have ever hoped for…it's just—"

"A lot."

She smiled gently at me. "Yeah."

I asked the question I really didn't want to. "Do you want me to back off?"

"Fuck no."

I blinked.

Her smile turned mischievous. "You think I don't know what *I've* got, baby?" she teased. "I'll take my romance whiplash any day."

"See?" I whispered. "How can I not love that?"

"And to think it was all because of ketchup and me yelling at you."

"Never say that I'm not a romantic, whiplash or otherwise." I leaned close and tugged her ponytail. "Just prepare yourself for the inevitability that I'm getting you ketchup for your anniversary present."

She huffed. "You know none of this makes any sense. Six years and ketchup is the driving force—"

"Since when does the world make sense?"

Lily wrinkled her nose, which I took to mean that she was conceding the point. Also, this just in, but, damn, she was cute, especially glaring up at me and saying, "You'd better not get me ketchup as an anniversary present."

"How about a beach vacation and *then* I give you ket—"

She rose up on her knees and kissed me.

And then, under clear skies and moonlight, a rented house

and our teammates behind us, the ocean in the distance, I kissed her back.

Thinking that the world might be fucked up, but at least I'd finally gotten my shit together.

All because Lily had pulled my head out of my ass.

So how couldn't I love her?

She was absolutely everything.

CHAPTER SEVENTEEN

Lily

IT WAS AFTER MIDNIGHT.

We'd been in the house for ten days.

And I thought I'd finally found it.

"I think I found it," I whispered to myself. Unnecessarily since I was staring at it. But, "Holy shit, I *think* I found it."

I scrolled down the website's page, clicked back through the file of shell companies and banks I'd been keeping ever since we'd settled in this house, having added the six churches we'd discovered from the list.

Six churches.

Six deacons each.

Each one researched to an inch of their life. We had tracked down every connection, every bank account, and now, I had one property that was held by a deacon. And when I tracked property taxes—for so many fucking properties—but when I'd gone through the last year of this property, I found *it*. Paid in January of this year and paid by a check.

And *that* check?

The top didn't list the deacon's name.

Instead, the name at the top was for another church.

A new church, the name of which I hadn't yet come across.

Quickly, I said fuck-all to fancy deep dives into the church's name—Verity—and just typed it into the search bar. And when I hit enter…

The top result was a stripped-down website, its background image being scales.

Overlaying a crescent moon.

And written in the curve of that moon…*Quod vero dicitur per comparationem.*

The truth is relative.

Just like the tattoo.

And when I clicked through, I found pictures of its members. Just right on those public pages, pictures of those deacons from the six churches, dotted with members of their flocks. All smiling huge like they were happy members of the same congregation.

The thirty-six members. Together.

I zoomed in. Every fucking hand had a tattoo.

Finally, a finite connection.

And an address…in Paris.

Less than ten hours from where we were.

"Holy shit," I whispered. "We found it. I found it!" I jumped up onto my feet, and yeah, my happy dance was in full swing when the light flicked on over my head.

I froze, blinking against the sudden glare.

Hannah grinned. "Sure can move, baby."

Would the floor just open up and swallow me whole? At least just until my cheeks stopped blazing and Hannah stopped smirking at me and—

"You found it?" she prompted.

My embarrassment faded because fuck it that she'd caught me dancing. I'd *found* it. Literally, I'd found the place that linked the churches, found a website we could dive deep into for more information, but more importantly, I'd found the place!

The place that tied them all together.

I rushed over to Hannah, hugged her tight. "I fucking found it!" I exclaimed. "It's in Paris, and we have to go. We have to go *now*. Finally, we're a step ahead of them. We can't wait. We've got to pack our shit and *go*."

"Show me what you have."

I dropped my arms, stepped back, and hurried to my computer.

And I showed her.

She kissed me hard when I'd finished. "Damn, baby. You fucking did it."

"*We* did it."

And Kenny was right.

The USB had been the key. One to the first door that led to a whole fucking hallway of doors, each one we'd had to pick the lock on to get through to the end.

But now we were there.

About fifteen minutes later, we had the house packed up.

And about two minutes after that, we were on the road.

———

"MOVE ON ONE," Hannah murmured into my ear. "Three. Two. *One!*"

I darted across the alley, pressing my body flat to the brick wall, holding my breath as I slid to the right, out of camera range.

"What do you see?"

Her voice was confident and assured, no hint at the danger that might lay ahead.

Which was why she was our leader.

Which was why I fucking loved her.

I paused at the corner of the building, gave in to my inner

squee (because she loved me back), but just as quickly, I pushed that aside, focusing on the job at hand.

Namely, infiltrating the building and finding some actual shit out.

We'd reconnoitered, watched, and waited. Documented the comings and goings.

And now it was time to go in.

The door we'd identified as the weak point was in sight, and we knew the plainclothes security guard would patrol by in thirty seconds.

"Leo," Hannah said. "You ready on those cameras?"

"On your mark," he replied.

"Jesse, you ready with that distraction?"

"Roger that."

"Linc?"

"Keeping watch. All players in their typical positions."

"Lil?"

"Ready, honey."

Not professional. Endearments should probably be held back from mission communications. But I loved the woman, and I was me, and so...*honey*.

Yeah, I was going into a potentially deadly situation with my girlfriend—eek!—on the com.

This was still my life.

So, I was living it as me.

Hannah better get on the ride, strap in, and hold the fuck on.

I wanted that vacation on the beach—even if it came with the bottle of ketchup.

"On one, baby."

Baby.

Baby.

"Fuck, I love you," I whispered.

"Three," Hannah said, "two, one. *Go*."

I went, sprinting to the door, sticking my pins in the lock, picking it, and moving inside, and the last words I heard before I slipped inside, shutting it behind me, were, "I love you, too."

———

IT LOOKED LIKE A NORMAL CHURCH.

It *looked* like those pictures from the blog—the stained glass, the woodwork, the altar and pews—only this church was bigger.

But…it felt wrong.

Quiet and unused, almost like it was a façade.

The air was almost stale, the space too quiet. "You getting this?" I whispered.

"Yes," Hannah said. "Stay sharp. This doesn't feel right."

I didn't answer.

I *couldn't* answer.

Because suddenly I wasn't alone.

Footsteps coming closer.

And…nowhere for me to hide.

"Code Black," I whispered, instantly telling the team that someone was approaching. They'd know to keep quiet on the coms and to move closer in case I needed backup. Even as I said that, I was flowing to the ground, using the shadows near the altar to blend into the space. I'd be fucked if all the lights went on, because there wasn't anywhere to hide, but I had to hope that my instincts about the front of the church being mostly for show purposes panned out.

I went still, regulated my breathing.

The footsteps grew closer.

Closer still.

Close enough that a bead of sweat trickled down my spine, and I was seriously regretting fighting to be the one to penetrate the building. Yeah, I was good at it and probably had the most experience picking locks and getting into places people didn't want me to get into, but I'd also fought like hell with Hannah about being the one to go headfirst into danger, fought so hard we had to have our first moderated-by-Linc discussion.

Because she was the team leader and thought that risk should always fall to her.

Because she'd finally given in to what was in her heart and we'd had a week of *us*.

And it was good.

And we both wanted that *good* to go on for the rest of our lives—

Those lives being long, and maybe not uneventful, but filled with good things like vacations on the beach and giant bottles of ketchup that were currently being shipped to my dropbox in Paris so I could give Hannah a hard time about her sense of romance.

I'd won the argument, obviously—or rather, Linc had cited my increased lock-picking and infiltrating skills as the reason for siding with me, and Hannah, though clearly not liking it, had lived up to the deal we'd struck in a bathroom several hundred miles south.

So now I was inside, and I was seconds away from being discovered by some really fucking bad guys, and I…

Was pissed.

So pissed.

Because I wanted Hannah and the beach (and frankly, the mountains—preferably a mountain lake since that was my jam a hell of a lot more than getting sand into all sorts of orifices… and yes, I apparently used the word *orifices* when my adrenaline was pumping). I wanted ketchup and to give her shit for not saving me fries.

I wanted this fucking mystery solved because I was tired of spending ten hours a day at a computer tracking down bastards who weren't making the world a better place, who were fucking it up royally, and who were taking my time away from that beach and lake and ketchup…and also from the other fuckers who were keen on making trouble in the world but because we'd all been so focused on the Confederate, we couldn't make trouble for *them*.

I wanted this done because I was tired of lagging one step behind and being shot and stabbed and having my car flipped when all I wanted to do was binge on candy bars and sleep.

I wanted this done…because I wanted to discover the connection to KTS, because I wanted to make sure the organization I worked for was clean, and if they were, then I was tired of being one step behind these people who were so capable of turning our agents…and because of that, always being that one step ahead.

I wanted…

The footsteps stuttered, as though the person walking had stutter-stepped.

As though that stutter-stepping had occurred because they had seen something. Something perhaps, like a person hiding in the shadows behind the altar and that person not being the fucking maid service giving the baseboards a wipe down.

Fuck.

Fuck.

"Steady," Hannah whispered in my ear.

I hadn't been about to bolt. I'd trained too hard and long to panic like that, but I *had* been focused more on the sense of foreboding than my surroundings, and Hannah's words snapped me back into them.

The footsteps began again, and I knew the camera that was strapped to my front was recording in night vision mode when I heard the inhale of breaths in my ear before the shadowy figure got near enough for me to see his face.

His. Face.

Joseph Cullins.

Hannah's father.

He looked like her. Same eyes. Same lips. Hints of the same nose, and maybe if the lights had been fully on and I wasn't crouching in shadows and had seen him on the sidewalk, his hair would have been Hannah's. But there plastered against the wall, a foreboding statue of Jesus my only cover, I didn't have a great view of the color of his short, well-groomed locks.

I just knew his vibe was…off.

Not exactly outright malice, but the waves of emotion radiating off him, filling the space…they were giving me serious Do Not Pass Go vibes. They were *giving* me get-the-fuck-out-and-come-back-with-a-fucking-tank-to-mow-down-this-sick-fucker vibes.

And consequently, not passing Go along the way.

He was also staring at the floor, and I didn't know why that was.

For a long moment, he didn't move…

And then he did…

CHAPTER EIGHTEEN

Hannah

"DO *NOT* GO DOWN THERE," I hissed, watching the feed of Lily's camera as she approached the door my father had disappeared down.

This being after he'd stopped and stared at the floor, then at the altar where Lil had been hiding (nearly giving me a fucking heart attack in the process and nearly having me send the whole team in a way that would get Lil out, but wouldn't be quiet and sneaky like we were attempting, a way that would ruin this fucking lead and blow our cover and probably make the Confederate scatter into the fucking shadows again...meaning that any work we had done to this point would be absolutely pointless).

Lily ignored me.

Obviously.

Because she reached out, carefully opened the door that blended so fucking well in with the wall that unless I'd just watched my father walk through it on the camera feed, I wouldn't have known it was there.

Then, still ignoring me, she slipped inside that door, closing it silently behind her.

I didn't like this.

Not one fucking bit.

I liked it even less when the feed immediately got a little staticky, and one glimpse through the monitor of the heavy-hewn stone walls, telling me why and telling me that the feed wouldn't get better if she descended the steps that were in front of her.

Dim light at the bottom of the stairs.

A wooden handle roughly installed into the stone, probably because my parents and the other deacons from the other churches weren't exactly spring chickens.

A fall down an old staircase made of cobblestone and not up to the American building code system (meaning tread length, slope, and rise height—and yes, I was focusing on building codes in order to not lose my fucking mind because Lil, because *my* woman, my team member who I was supposed to be looking after wasn't listening to me.

And because she *wasn't* listening to me (something, by the way, that she'd never fucking done before…at least not on a mission), she was putting herself in danger.

"I'm going," was all she whispered before she began down that staircase, and doing it quick.

"You made me promise to pause and consider—"

Her feet kept moving down the stairs.

Fuck.

I knew she moved so rapidly not because she was worried that I'd send in the cavalry (I would, she knew that, but only when it wouldn't hopefully put her in more danger and blow our lead), but because she was out in the open and vulnerable. If someone came in behind her through the door, if someone tried to exit that space and wanted to do it using the staircase, there wasn't any cover.

She was out in the open.

At risk.

So I didn't snap in her earpiece to get the fuck out of there. I didn't barrel in and risk exposing her.

I stood there in an apartment across the street from the church, watching the monitor and thinking that I hoped my woman was into sex that was a little bit freaky, because I wasn't opposed to tying her to my bed and turning her ass pink.

My breath held as she descended the stairs in quick, efficient movements.

Released when she reached the bottom of the case and moved forward carefully, clearing the space, finding a bit of cover she could retreat to if necessary—this being a narrow alcove that wasn't ideal for a lot of reasons, but it was something and it reminded me that Lily was good at this, good at her job, an excellent agent who—this moment aside—didn't take unnecessary risks.

Then she began creeping forward.

The space was old, and I could almost feel the cold and damp drifting through the air, even through the monitor, but the hallway was short, and it didn't go on for long. Maybe ten feet of stone walls on either side of the hall before it opened into a huge atrium.

The feed went clear.

Crystal *fucking* clear.

Like instead of being in a several hundred-year-old church, she had just walked into a modern office building with the best internet on the planet.

Then I wasn't thinking about connectivity because I was processing the images on my screen.

And my mouth fell open at the sheer size of it.

Three—no, *four*—stories sprawled overhead, each brightly lit with modern-looking lighting and glass and metal railings closing off each level. Staircases interspersed the space, hung from steel cables that seemed oddly at home with the rustic stone they were fastened into. Each level had...cubicles.

No, not cubicles.

But, yes, workstations, the glowing monitors present even from a distance.

Hundreds of people could work here.

Hundreds.

It didn't really hit me until then, how big the Confederate was. But seeing all those empty workstations?

Then it hit me and hit me hard.

How did that many people come to work in an old building like that without being seen on our reconnaissance?

But I didn't have time to process that question because Lil was moving swiftly and quietly through the space, darting through the bands of light that highlighted the huge central space that was filled with row after row of pews, each with a prayer book resting on the seat. Pausing to pick up one of those books. I listened to her clothing rustle as she shoved it in the pocket of her cargos.

Then moving, still moving, and doing it in a way that was fast and silent and still managed to get us footage.

I think she heard it the same time I did in the control room.

Voices.

"Careful," I whispered.

She didn't respond, but I know she heard because her breath whispered across the microphone. A slow exhale, just like she'd done before when she was taking cover behind the altar.

Then she was moving down another hallway.

This one stone like the first, the feed going staticky again.

Another door.

Heavy and ornately carved, and…voices echoing through the other side.

She reached forward, fingers wrapping around the knob—

It turned under her hand, swung out, nearly colliding with her body.

I stifled a curse, watched as she jumped back, sliding behind the door as it opened.

Two men walked out, and because of her position behind the door, it was impossible to see more than that except to hear their voices—numbering two, to hear they were male. And that was it, then they were walking down the hall and Lil was moving, slipping through the door before it shut, and entering a meeting space.

That was filled with people.

Fuck.

"Retreat," I hissed.

Because those people?

Every last person sitting in a wooden high-backed chair, a la some stupid King Arthur reenactment. I didn't have time to count, but there were a lot and based on our research—six deacons from six churches—I could assume there were actually thirty-six chairs, and they were currently occupied by thirty-four people.

And because two were empty and presumably belonging to the men in the hallway, I could suppose that the chairs wouldn't be empty for long.

Her retreat failed when one set of eyes came up, noticed her, and then more joined the first, and more, until the entire space went quiet and the gazes on her numbered more than I had the capacity to count at that moment.

Lily tried.

Valiantly.

She pulled out her phone, spoke in a thick British accent, "Can you help me find the…" She named a nearby tourist site.

Maybe it would have worked if she'd been discovered upstairs or even in the atrium.

But stumbling upon a meeting down a staircase, through a dimly lit hallway, across a giant atrium filled with workstations, through another dimly lit hallway, and then stumbling into that meeting of the dumbass King Arthur chairs?

Not ideal.

"No?" she asked, backing toward the door. "That's all right then." More inching. "I'll just see myself out and—"

"Linc, Leo, Jess?" I breathed into our comms.

"Already moving," Linc murmured.

Suicide to send my team in when we'd be outnumbered almost six to one, when we didn't know what these people could do, what weapons they had. What backup might be lurking in the spaces Lil hadn't yet checked.

We'd experienced some of the Confederate's firepower.

I knew it was dangerous, that *they* were dangerous.

And that was why I knew it was suicide to send in my team.

But we didn't leave our people behind, and even if we did, *I* couldn't have left Lily in that situation.

Even though she hadn't listened.

Even though this entire mission was fucked.

Because I loved her.

And fuck it. I was going in, too.

I made sure the monitor was still recording, grabbed a few extra guns, and then I hit the staircase, moved through the shadows, and slid into the same door that she'd picked a half hour before.

Leo and Linc came through the front.

Jesse slid in behind me.

Then we moved, still listening to Lily trying to bluff her way out of this.

"No really," she said, still full on Brit. "That's all right. Obviously, I took a wrong turn and interrupted. I'll just go back and retrace my steps."

"Lilian Cartwright."

A cold voice. A cold female voice I knew in the bottom of my soul.

"I know you're not stupid. Don't presume me to be either. I've read your file. I've read *all* of your files. I know you." A sniff. "And your sins."

Leo shot me a look, and I confirmed it with a nod. That voice belonged to my mother. Who had confirmed what we already knew.

They had someone inside KTS.

"Move," I whispered.

Rifle out, Leo waited for Linc to yank open the door, cleared the space in front of them, and moved in through the doorway. The rest of us filed in, taking his back, moving quickly down the staircase.

All while I listened to Lily.

Talking now, but having dropped the Brit.

"You're Hannah's mom."

"I don't have a daughter." A pause. "Now, dear," she said, and though the endearment was there, her tone didn't change from cold, from so fucking cold that it was a dagger of ice through my heart. "Since we have company, we're going to have to catch up later. For now, you're going to have to come with me."

"I—"

A scuffle.

Then a grunt.

We were through the atrium, into the second hallway.

Not moving cautiously.

Not moving slowly.

We reached the door.

It was locked. It was heavy. Didn't matter. Linc scooted forward, slapped a band of explosive near the handle. "Eyes," he warned.

I slammed them shut.

I saw the flash behind those closed lids.

Then I opened them, my team, presumably, had too because we moved forward as one. Linc kicking the door open, Leo at his shoulder, Jesse and me bringing up the rear.

Prepared to face thirty-four deacons and whatever weapons or guards they might have summoned.

We hauled ass into that room…

And found it completely empty.

And while I was desperately searching for the exit, for the door they must have taken Lily through…the world exploded.

CHAPTER NINETEEN

LILY

TIME: *0346hrs*
  Location: Fuck if she knew
  Situation: FUBAR

THE DIGITAL CLOCK on the wall was really not helpful.

I didn't need to know what time they were dragging a knife over my skin, digging the tip in a way that was designed to draw out the pain.

The hand passed in front of my face, a tattoo inked on the space between thumb and forefinger, a flash of black ink—a crescent moon, a set of scales, a line written in Latin, and I forgot about how long I'd spent studying that fucking tattoo, tracking down the deacons, only to get caught because I'd gone in too fast.

Gotten caught because of a boot scuff on the floor of the church back in Paris.

Back because I had no clue where I was.

Only that one moment I'd been inching toward the door, wanting the fuck away from Mary Cullins and the maniacal look in her eyes, and the next I'd felt a presence at my spine.

I'd gotten one good lick in before the world went black.

Then I'd woken up here.

With the digital clock telling me the time, no windows, no sense of whether it had been minutes or hours or days that had passed, though I'd had the sense that it had been hours.

Now however, I'd been awake and unconscious so many times, even trying to keep track of the hours that I'd seen on that fucking digital clock and I didn't know how many days had passed.

Just that Mary Cullins with her maniacal eyes had been in and out. Not wielding the knife but supervising the "cleansing."

Me being the one who needed said cleansing by being beat to shit, sliced to shit, and my blood leaking out until it stained the grout on the tile floor crimson.

And all the while as she supervised my *cleansing* Joseph Cullins had stood at her shoulder.

In silent support.

Because it was clear to everyone in the room that Mary was the one in charge.

Everyone I'd seen had deferred to her.

Everyone.

I didn't have time to focus on the irony of a female cult leader who was hard into a religion that typically had a woman's place in the home.

Because the pain began again, and as much as I tried to stay in my mind, tried to focus on the weeks and months we'd spent tracking down the Confederate, the agony of that knife dragging through my skin—*through*, not over—yanked me out of my brain.

Away from the digital clock.

Away from the thoughts of my team, my love for Hannah,

my parents—who God, would be so fucking upset that I'd gone and gotten myself killed.

That pain yanked me firmly out of my brain and into my body.

And…it hurt.

So fucking *much*.

Not just from the agony of that blade slicing through my skin, nor the dripping knife wounds.

But from the gunshot wound in my thigh.

The broken wrist that was encased in handcuffs, meaning the metal dug into those shattered bones every time I moved, spreading a brand-new wave of shooting pain through me with every cut.

Bruises covered my naked skin.

I had long since been stripped of my body armor, my protective clothing, my boots. My gun and knife, even the hidden blade sewn into the seam of my bra, was gone.

It was cold. Frost condensing our breaths. The walls damp with water droplets, the moisture gathering everywhere, even coating the plastic covering of the digital clock, making the three look like it was dripping down, melting like some sick Salvador Dali painting.

Naked. Bound. Injured. My blood coating the floor.

And alone.

Well, alone because it was just me and my kidnappers, all of whom didn't bother to hide their faces.

Because I wouldn't make it out of here alive.

They knew it.

I knew it.

Because I was trained to be a KTS agent, trained to protect myself, to hack computers, to use any and all weapons at my disposal, and to *never stop fighting*. But I'd been trained to do that knowing I had a team at my back, that I wouldn't be left behind, that I wouldn't be alone.

But my team was dead

I was alone.

I was still going to fight, to never stop.

I was still going to die.

———

THE DOOR CREAKED OPEN.

Mary made her appearance, a wicked—ironic, wasn't it?—smile on her face.

She held up the prayer book. "Shall we begin with today's lessons?"

I could barely lift my head, let alone come back with some snark.

Not when the last time she'd been in this room, she'd shown me pictures of my teammates...or their remains anyway.

Burned and battered.

Hannah's boot.

That was what had gotten me. Her boot, the right one she always laced a little funny, skipping the second from the top eyelet before going through the top one and pulling it tight.

Sitting on its side amongst the rubble.

That was when I knew.

That was when it got a lot harder to fight.

One of the men who always surrounded her scooted forward and pulled a chair up for her. And she opened the prayer book, began reading.

The problem with this wasn't the prayers.

It wasn't the reading.

It was what happened when she *stopped* reading. If I didn't answer the questions she posed to me exactly right, if I didn't repeat the verses exactly back to her...I earned more cleansing.

In the form of my blood.

And honestly, I didn't know how I had any blood left in my body.

Or a body that still worked, that managed to clot, that

wasn't riddled with infection or hypothermic. Though, I supposed it was both of the final two.

I was colder and colder every moment I was awake, and those lucid moments were coming fewer and farther in between. I was losing feeling in my fingers, my toes, and the broken wrist...I was worried if I somehow got out of here that I wouldn't be able to use it again.

"Why?" I asked, interrupting her.

Which would normally have gotten me another knife, maybe if I was really rude and bad with my timing, another gunshot wound.

Today, she maybe took pity on me.

Or maybe she just knew how close to the edge I was.

Her eyes—hazel like Hannah's—met mine. "Why am I doing this to you?" Cold. Unaffected.

"No," I said, voice so damned raspy because as much as I had tried over the last days to not cry out, to not scream, I'd failed on that. "Why did you do that to Hannah?"

A flicker in those eyes.

Fury? Guilt? Regret? Disgust?

Maybe if I'd been at full capacity, I would have been able to read her. As it was, I was barely conscious. But I had to know.

Because if I got out of here, I needed to be able to tell Hannah.

Who's dead! So, it doesn't fucking matter.

I needed to know for myself then, because this woman had turned all sorts of wonderful away, shit on it, wounded it deep.

And Hannah had gotten a couple weeks of accepting she could be loved for who she was inside.

So many years of suffering for so little.

Mary's face transformed, going full sneer, the ice completely gone.

"Hannah was an abomination."

"Then I'm one, too," I rasped, "because I love her."

Fury across her face, a nod to the man at her right elbow,

and even though I braced, the knife sinking into my leg still had me screaming.

Mary stood up. "She needs to be cleansed."

"Why?" I repeated.

She whirled back. "I told you, she is no daughter of mine, and unless you repent, you'll earn a place beside her in the ground."

"I will always be what I am," I said. "And that's someone who tries to be good and fights for what's right. Who loves a woman who was the best person I'd ever met and—"

Mary snatched the knife from the man beside her, plunged it into my stomach.

I screamed.

She leaned close. "I have worked for *years* to cleanse this world. I have fought, and I have sacrificed, and I won't have some fucking dyke ruin that for me. The pieces are in place. The world is going to know what the Confederate should be and—"

The wall blew open.

Not the door. But the entire wall just fucking exploded, sending rocks and debris flying in every direction.

Mary screamed, but only for one beat before she was face down on the floor, hands zip-tied behind her back, the three men accompanying her down just as quickly.

"Lily," Olive said, diving toward me. She covered my body as more people entered the room, as there were several scuffles that ultimately ended up with more people zip-tied on the floor next to Mary and her boy toys.

My breath hissed out of me as she pushed off.

Then it appeared she got a good look at my face, my body, and her expression went blank.

"Fuck," I whispered, going for a joke, "I look *that* bad?"

She gently smoothed back my hair, continued surveying me. When she reached the handcuffs, she turned and ordered, "Bolt cutters."

I managed to focus, saw that Laila was there and Dan, Ava,

and Ryker.

Ryker's eyes were furious, but he nodded at Olive, disappeared out the opening they'd blown in the wall. Olive, meanwhile, had retrieved her pack and was going to work on the worst of my injuries, and truthfully, I would have preferred to be unconscious for those particular ministrations.

Unfortunately, I didn't get that.

And a few minutes later, Ryker was back, holding the bolt cutters. He moved behind me, and I held in my groan when my broken wrist was jostled, and then another when the tension increased on the cuffs.

"Sorry, honey," he murmured.

More pressure. A snap.

Then the chain had been cut, my arms were free.

Another cut, and my ankles followed suit.

"We've gotta move—" Olive began, but Laila knelt in front of me.

"How many more?" she asked.

"I saw at least twelve in my time here." A nod, her gaze going to Ryker and Ava. "Let's clear this—"

I reached out with my uninjured hand, caught her wrist when she would have moved off. "She said"—I flicked my eyes toward Mary—"that pieces were in place, that the world would know—"

Laila bent. "Nukes," she murmured. "We intercepted them this morning."

I inhaled sharply, and fuck, but that was painful. "Be careful."

A gentle hand on my shoulder. "We found them, Lil. Thanks to you. We found them all, and they're secure, and we've moved on every Confederate location—"

I frowned.

She patted my shoulder. "Debrief later. Just know Skye and I hit pay dirt, and add in what you found and Rochester's USB, and we broke it. Finally, we broke it."

Relief slid through me, and I nodded. "I—"

Gunfire rang out, and Laila spun, face serious as Ryker and Ava pushed to the door. "We'll clear the place. Olive, you and Dan get Lily safe."

Then they were gone. More gunshots were exchanged. Sirens sounded, and haze intruded on the edges of my vision.

Dan bent by my side. "Ready, Lil?" he asked gently. "We'll get you out of here."

"I can walk." I tried to prove this by pushing to my feet, and I made it.

Then nearly ate shit because I was wounded and had been shot and I was still actively bleeding, and my blood was staining the grout on the floor.

Dan swept me up before I hit the ground.

Olive grabbed the pack, pulled out her gun, and led the way.

Dan, embarrassingly, carried me out through that hole in the wall, out through another hole in another wall, and then through a series of rooms. *And* up a staircase, through a winding set of hallways, and finally out into the night air.

The sun was up.

The weather was beautiful.

There were police and military, SUVs and squad cars scattered around like candy. Dan started to carry me to an ambulance—

"No," I said. "I—"

"You're bad, sweetheart," he said carefully. "You need a hospital, and you need it quick."

I knew that. I could feel that.

But…there was something, something on the edges of my memory. Something I needed to tell him, something I'd seen—someone I'd seen who'd been standing at Mary's shoulder.

Someone who—

I lost it.

And then I lost consciousness.

CHAPTER TWENTY

Hannah

SECOND-DEGREE BURNS ON MY ARMS.

Six stitches on my temple.

Another twelve in my thigh.

A tweaked knee. A broken finger.

But I was alive.

And so were Linc, Jesse, and Leo. And so was Lily.

Thinking they'd taken Lily from Paris, we'd gone to the church in Berlin, found an underground chamber that was apparently standard in all Confederate churches (along with weapons, tech, bunkers, and a plethora of fucking insane followers who wanted to cleanse the world).

Cleanse meaning eliminating anyone who wasn't straight and white.

Nazis.

We were dealing with fucking neo-Nazis.

And my mother was the ringleader of them all. She'd spent the last two decades taking that cult-like church I'd grown up in and expanding it. First, by deposing the deacon I'd listened to throughout my entire childhood, saying he was too liberal (him!) and morphing the church into something that was more tyrannical than puritanical, and its members got off on it.

Which meant her power grew and expanded, and eventually she found other like-minded churches to join with. Expanding the leadership, and with it the access to funds and new members, but deftly keeping her position on top.

Because there hadn't been thirty-six chairs around that table.

When we'd gone back through the footage, we'd been able to see that there had actually been thirty-seven.

One, just a little bit fancier than the rest. One, my fucking *mother's* chair.

Because she was supposedly closer to God.

How did I know all of this?

Because I'd just left the observation room, and I'd been *observing* Laila interviewing my mother. Who'd shared enough, and shared it wide and freely, not because she was looking for a deal, but because she'd been cursing everyone far and wide, and in that talk of brimstone and going to Hell, we'd gotten information.

My dad was talking.

And the shit they were in was deep, involved multiple juris-dictions, governments, international agencies. Their cover, their hidden organization, was blown so fucking wide that it wouldn't stay underground.

Thirty-six deacons.

Thirty-six locations breached.

Their entire leadership arrested and hundreds of people beneath them. It was on the news. It was on the internet.

It was official.

The Confederate were fucked.

And also exposed.

Now, however, I'd seen enough. Our work was done. My family was more fucked than I'd ever imagined, and...I didn't care.

I was alive.

Lily was alive.

It was done.

My past was in ashes. Where it belonged.

So, I walked out of the KTS base and headed straight to the hospital.

———

LILY WAS STILL out when I got to the hospital.

No surprise when one considered the broad scope of her injuries. It was lucky she was here and breathing.

They'd had her for a week.

I would never forgive myself for that, never stop trying to make it up to her.

Hurt because of *me*.

"No, I'm not," she whispered.

I blinked, realized I'd said that out loud.

And she was awake.

Bruised, battered, but alive.

"How?" she asked, the question a hoarse whispered.

"When your GPS didn't ping,"—we all had chips implanted on our bodies somewhere, but they weren't foolproof, case in point, they didn't work well through thick stone or concrete walls like where Lily had been held, in one of those bunkers in a Confederate church outside of Paris—"we followed the prayer book. We found the one you grabbed from the atrium, discarded in the alley. It had your prints on it," I added when she frowned. "And we went through it, page by fucking disgusting page, and when that didn't bring anything obvious, we tracked the printers who made it."

"Smart," she whispered.

I reached for her hand, held it gingerly. "I get all my tips from the smartest woman I know."

Lil smiled, and it was a glorious thing.

"From there," I said, sliding my chair closer, carefully weaving our fingers together (those of her uninjured hand), "we tracked all the shipments, and when we realized what they led to, we made this shit big, called in every favor and team, including me kissing KTS's upper echelon's asses." I chuckled but cut it short when her brows drew together.

"What?" I asked, frowning.

She tugged her hand free, rubbed her temple. "Nothing," she muttered. "Or nothing I can remember at this moment."

I sank into the chair, gently smoothed back her hair. "You want to rest?"

"I *want* to hear the rest of it," she said.

"You really want to hear how I think I may have given up all my PTO for the next several centuries, so we might have to wait a while for that beach vacation—"

"A.k.a. ketchup," she teased.

Teased.

Thank fuck she was teasing me.

I sucked in a breath, knew my voice was nowhere near steady and everywhere near shaky, when I said, "I'll survive."

Fingers on my cheek. "I know you will."

And we stayed there like that for a long moment, my eyes burning, Lily's glistening, our gazes saying everything our voices couldn't in that moment.

Love and relief.

Terror and grief.

And over.

It was finally over.

"Now," she murmured, "you need to tell me the rest."

"Not much more to tell," I admitted. "Somehow despite all the links, we managed to both keep the larger mission quiet and were able to move on all the delivery locations at once. Probably because Laila, Skye, and I all worked off-grid until we'd gathered all the information. Then we called in favors, got everyone on board, and coordinated everything within six hours."

A fucking miracle that was.

"I'm impressed."

"You should be," I said lightly. "It was mostly your work."

She *pfted*. Then winced, so I reached down for the morphine button, pushing it before she could argue that she didn't need it. "Damn," she muttered, holding her side, "this sucks." I set the button down, and she glared. "Also, don't think I missed you giving me drugs to knock me out." A beat. "I'll kick your ass for it later."

I grinned, pressed a kiss to her forehead. "No pain, baby." I straightened. "No more pain for you. *Ever*."

"I don't think—"

"And for the record," I added before she could get a full head of steam behind her, "Linc is springing you from here tomorrow, and then you'll have the ministrations of Olive *and* him to contend with. So, good luck with that."

A small smile, her lips tipping up, lids growing heavy, drifting closed. "Throwing me to the wolves already?"

I tucked a strand of hair behind her ear. "Never."

"How?"

The drugs were hitting her so hard she didn't remember what I'd just said?

"I just told you, baby."

"No," she whispered, lids peeling back, eyes filled with tears. "How are you alive? I saw"—a tear slid free—"I saw pictures and you guys were—"

"Doctored," I told her quickly. "There was an explosion, but other than a few scratches and bruises, we're okay."

I left off the broken bones.

My mother had begun to talk as well, and she'd mentioned the pictures, along with the great joy it brought her to wreak havoc on Lily's heart.

"They were just another way to punish us, to try to break you down."

She got quiet. Then, so softly, I had to lean close to hear, "It almost worked."

Fuck. My heart squeezed hard. "You were still breathing when we got there, baby," I said, "So, no, it didn't almost work. You fought, and you survived, and the groundwork you laid—not to mention the prayer book you managed to leave for us to find after we'd made it out of those tunnels"—the tunnels we'd discovered as we'd dug ourselves out, tunnels that led to an exit several blocks over in a parking garage. Which was why we hadn't noticed the comings and goings during our reconnaissance—"and you know what the first thing we saw when we'd managed to dig our way out?"

She shook her head.

"That book. With your prints on it."

"I guess lady luck was looking out for me," she whispered.

"My *lady* had nothing to do with luck and everything to do with skill."

Her lids flashed open, laughter dancing through her eyes as she winced. "Now *that* was a bad line."

I shrugged, so fucking thankful to see that amusement on her face. "I live to please."

More laughter, this time filling the air. But only for a second. Because then she winced, and the laughter cut off and she glared. "No making me laugh. Especially when I feel high as fuck."

"Okay, baby. No more laughing." I smoothed back her hair. "Sleep now."

"Okay," she whispered.

I turned down the light, kept smoothing back her hair.

She let her eyes close, her breathing slowed, and I thought she'd fallen asleep, she was so still. Then her lids peeled back, and she held my gaze. "There's something I'm not remembering," she whispered, her words coming slow and slurred. "It's all so fuzzy and confusing and—"

She broke off, struggling for a few moments.

"It'll come, baby," I said when that struggle was fruitless. "I promise, it'll come." I brushed my thumb lightly over her bottom lip. "But for now, you need to rest up and heal so we can hit that beach."

Her mouth curved under my thumb.

"Beach," she murmured. "And ketchup."

"Damn right."

Her smile held. "More of a mustard fan, myself."

"Oh, the humanity," I deadpanned.

A giggle.

I chuckled, held her hand as she slid into sleep.

And I did it thinking I was the luckiest motherfucker ever.

Then that I was even luckier when she breathed, "Love you."

CHAPTER TWENTY-ONE

LILY

OKAY, the verdict was in.

One medic was bad.

Two was too many.

I was one hour of Linc and Olive fussing over me away from losing my absolute shit.

Absolute. Shit.

One more *just let me check this bandage to make sure you're healing*, one more *I need to take your vitals another time so I can log it in your chart*, one more *I'll help you to the bathroom*.

For fuck's sake, I could wipe my own ass.

And yeah, did it take me a fucking decade to get to the toilet and back? Fuck yes, it did. Did I also have to hold back copious amounts of groans and grimaces as I did so, and perhaps even more when I had to lower my ass onto the toilet seat?

No surprise that the answer to both of those was also yes.

Still, I could do it.

A woman needed *some* standards.

A knock on the door had me looking up. Hannah was

leaning against the doorway at the KTS base outside of Atlanta, arms crossed, my fantasy come to life, and that included the soft way she was staring at me.

"You have *got* to get me out of here," I begged.

"Linc says he'll spring you in the morning."

Groaning, I dropped my head back to the pillows. That was hours away. That was plenty of hours for them to keep going all *one more* on me. "Sweet Christ. You have *got* to save me from this."

"Sorry, baby," she said, dropping her arms and crossing into the room. "But I'm with Linc on this one. I didn't almost lose you to have you rush your recovery."

"They practically bathed me in Olive's secret healing sauce," I muttered. "I feel better than I have in ages."

"Is that why you can't even lower yourself onto the toilet?" she asked dryly.

I narrowed my eyes.

"Love you," she said lightly, knowing she'd won. The fucking stink.

I sniffed.

She grinned.

"You're a pain in my ass," I continued with the muttering.

"Damned right I am."

A scowl, which just had her grin expanding, and it was so fucking beautiful to see her doing that, which was why I could pretend to be annoyed (pretend at Hannah, that was). Because I was definitely irritated at the combined power of Team Linco—side note, worst couples name ever. Also, side note, I was not currently at the top of my shit-giving game considering I'd been sliced, shot, broken, and on a months' long mission to try and solve this thing with the Confederate, but I'd be back up to my old standards of shit-giving soon (and step one of that would be coming up with a really awesome couples name I could torment them with for eternity).

Okay…

Even with Linc and Olive, it was pretend.

Because I loved them and they loved me and were protective and awesome and…I was going stir crazy, but I'd take it.

The Confederate was done.

We could get back to work.

Finally.

Well, *finally,* after a beach vacation and ketchup and a mountain lake and…me being able to wipe my own ass without smothering groans.

"Come over here," I grumbled, "and watch a movie with me. And not in that damned chair either." More grumbled. "In bed next to me, holding me close, and watching…"

I trailed off, mostly because she was suddenly next to my bed, toeing of her boots and gingerly pulling me against her chest. "Watching…" she prompted, and frankly, it took me a minute to catch my breath after she gave me that so freely, so easily.

I enjoyed the cuddle, the moment of just being in her arms.

I knew it would be burned on my soul forever.

Then I gave it to her—the title of the movie, that was—knowing that she would give that to me, too, even though she hated the film.

Knew she gave it to me, not just because I was recuperating and could pull the trump movie card. She gave it to me because I knew she would give me anything she could.

Because of ketchup and concrete that had been chipped slowly away. Because of visions of beaches and mountain lakes and a future that wasn't shadowed by the past.

She said she was okay about how shit went down with her mom.

I knew she wasn't.

I knew that would take time. I knew it was going to hit her hard, just like I knew we would need to have multiple conversations about it in the years ahead.

But that was the point.

We had *years*.

Just like I knew she'd watch this movie with me many more times over those years. Because even though she hated it, she knew I loved it.

So, she'd give it.

That was what love was.

And I knew she loved me to Mars and back when she clicked on the TV hanging on the wall opposite my bed, turned on that movie—my favorite, her most-hated—and then she just kissed the top of my head, snuggled in, and held on to me for the wild ride that was...

Die Hard.

"Best Christmas movie ever," I murmured, pressing a kiss to her jaw.

"It's June," she murmured back.

"Same difference."

A snort. A squeeze.

And then we settled in to watch the best movie of all time.

———

I WAS ALONE, dozing after the movie and the giant slab of chocolate cake Hannah had brought me from the mess when it happened.

Baseball was playing on TV.

Mostly because it was boring as hell, but I'd fallen asleep—gasp, I knew—during the greatest movie of all time, so I wasn't tired, but I knew I needed a full night's sleep so I'd be running optimum speed when it came to convincing Linc to spring me from this joint in the morning.

Because of that, I'd put on the thing I found most boring in the world, convinced Hannah to go sleep in her bed (she actually needed some real rest, too, considering she was healing from her injuries—bruises and scratches my ass—and she'd been pushing it taking care of me), and I'd lain there in the uncomfortable hospital bed, determined to find some shuteye.

Normally, I was good at this.

Normally, this was totally doable.

Sleep when I could, snatch it when I could.

But I'd slept *so fucking much* the last week that it was proving impossible.

So I was lying there, eyes closed, when footsteps echoed in the doorway. And, thinking it was Hannah coming to check on me, worrying like she'd done over the last week, I pretended that I was sleeping.

Fingers on my forehead.

I still didn't move.

Then fingers on my throat.

Wrapping *around* my throat.

I choked, my eyes flying open, my hands scrabbling at his.

At his.

Because then I *remembered*.

Who had been behind Mary in that room several times during my *cleansings*.

Who'd been in my room…unfortunately, just not when my rescue showed up.

Jeff.

Who had been all in on cleansing me, who'd particularly liked using the blade.

"Bitch," he hissed, squeezing tighter and unprepared for the assault, already black was edging into my vision. "Fucking *bitch*. I had it worked out. I was *there*. No one knew it was *me* that was giving the information, and then you fucked it all up for me. I was *in*. I was fucking perfect, had the best fucking golden parachute on the planet and you"—his hands clenched even more fiercely—"you couldn't let it go. You had to fuck me over."

Super helpful timing that *now* I remembered him in the room with Mary.

And as my air ran out, I also remembered that he'd been paired up with Kenny for a few missions—reports I'd read. Reports I'd filed away in my mental memory bank but reports that had appeared to have no connection.

Except perhaps that it had helped him pick a target.

Since I was now remembering *all* the things, since all the pieces were coming into place, I recalled Hannah mentioning Jeff and his team going off on another mission so had been unavailable for the second push of the investigation in Paris.

I also remembered that he'd been on base when Daniel had been murdered a few months ago, when someone somehow got past all our security measures.

Clearly, he'd helped the person who'd conducted the hit get in.

Oh, and his target of the Moldovan Five had somehow died. Not ours, not Laila's, not Skye's.

Just Jeff's.

Helped along, certainly based on this new information—that new information being that he was in the infirmary, at my bedside, currently helping *me* along.

I tucked my chin against his hold, tried to get some space so I could breathe.

I wasn't very successful.

But the only good thing about choking was that it wasn't a fast death.

If Jeff had brought a gun, if he'd decided to put a bullet in my brain, I would have been fucked. As it was, I barely had enough air to snake a hand down...

And press the emergency button.

An alarm would go to the nurse's station, and since those nurses were all KTS agents, all had kickass hand-to-hand combat skills, I knew that I'd be getting some help, and that help would be coming soon.

I...just...needed...to...hang—

The noise that filled the room penetrated that heavy fog that was pressing in on my mind.

It was part growl, part scream, part...inhuman keel.

And then the pressure around my neck faded. I snapped back into my bed, my body. Sucked in a breath. One more. Two more. Another gave me the energy to shove the blanket back. One more had my legs out of bed, bare feet hitting the floor. I was weak as hell and still healing, so standing wasn't fun, neither was rushing.

But Jeff was the mole, the traitor, the fucker who'd betrayed us.

So, I'd help, I'd fight, I'd—

Snap.

Jeff's lifeless body hit the ground.

Hannah was behind him, her eyes wild, her hands still lifted from where she'd snapped his neck.

Her gaze came to mine. "Lil?" she whispered.

I didn't think. I ignored the weakness, the pain, the stiffness. I closed the distance between us and threw myself into her arms.

She wrapped me tightly in them, buried her face in my hair.

That wasn't the most comfortable, but I wasn't going to complain.

Not when I had my Hannah.

"Him?" she whispered, as the room became crowded with people, the alarm I'd hit clearly having summoned enough backup that even if Hannah hadn't been there, I would have been good.

"Him," I whispered in agreement.

"Everything?" she asked.

"The final piece," I said in answer.

She exhaled, closed her eyes and when she opened them, the crazed expression had gone.

"Come on," she said, lifting me into her arms, bypassing the crowd, ignoring them, just as she ignored the body on the floor.

Questioning looks that turned to understanding when they spotted Jeff. Understanding and rage and relief.

Because we would finally be able to do our job.

Because we'd solved it.

Because…it was done.

Her long strides ate up the hallways that led to our quarters. To *my* quarters. "I'm moving in," she announced, slapping her palm on the panel and unlocking my door.

"Okay."

She strode inside, still giving orders. "Or you're moving into my room."

"Okay, honey."

She set me on the bed. "Or—"

"Hannah, my love, *okay,*" I said, fierce now that I had assumed a reclined position again. "I'm there or you're here, or hell, maybe we'll knock down the wall between our rooms and make this place a giant suite."

Glazed hazel eyes clearing, her fingers coming to my cheek, gently stroking. "Okay, baby."

She straightened, spent a few minutes fussing over the pillows and blankets, spreading some bruise cream on what I knew were the shape of Jeff's hands already appearing on my throat.

Because her expression went murderous as she did so.

Because she forced a mug of hot tea on me to ease the pain in my throat.

Because her fingers as she spread that salve were beyond gentle.

I loved that she worried, that she cared, that she'd exposed her big heart to the world, but in particular, I loved that she'd given that big, generous heart to *me.*

It was mine to protect.

Which was why I was me, would continue to be me. Because in that moment, she needed my special blend of Lily humor.

Light to wash out dark.

Joy to focus on living, on the future, instead of the past.

"So," I began with forced cheerfulness, "all I had to do to get out of the infirmary was—"

Her eyes narrowed. "Don't say it."

"Get—"

"*Don't* say it."

"A beautiful, prickly on the outside, kind-hearted on the inside woman to fall for me."

One second, there were sparks in those hazel eyes.

The next, there was humor.

Oh, and there was love, too. That special brand of courageous Hannah Love that she'd gifted me. *Only* me.

It was mine.

Forever.

And I was never looking back.

Not even if my parents somehow crashed this room with a bouquet of balloons, a Polaroid, and giant smiles.

Or maybe, it was that I couldn't wait until they did.

Because I was gifting her *my* special brand of Lily Love.

And I knew she'd keep it safe.

Protected.

Cherished.

Forever.

CHAPTER TWENTY-TWO

EPILOGUE, One Year Later

Hannah

I SAT ON THE BEACH, watching the sun rise over crystal clear blue waters and wondering why in the fuck-all I'd thought it had been a good idea to go on this vacation with Lily's parents.

We rarely got vacation.

This was our first time with sand—or well, with tropical sand beneath our toes when we weren't working a mission.

It was bathing suits (thank fuck Lily loved herself some bikinis) and cocktails on the beach. It was eating slowly by candlelight under the sticky air. It was lying in the air-conditioned hotel room, celebrating Lily accepting my ring and talking about ridiculous wedding plans.

Including adopting a dog so we could train it to carry a ring on a little pillow on its back.

Either that or a parakeet. Or maybe a pigeon.

It was speaking our vows in French or Italian or some other language of love.

It was…a hundred other things that were pure Lily.

Bright and filled with joy and always making me smile, making me laugh.

And…making me not agree to *any* of them. I just wanted Lily and I to make it official. I didn't care if she wore a dress or combat boots. It'd be cool if our friends could come, her parents. But it'd also be cool if it were just us and some Elvis impersonator and some paid witnesses.

I *really* didn't care.

Lily, no surprise, aside from busting my balls—or lack thereof—about carrier pigeons, had copious plans.

All of which she'd shared with her mom about ten seconds after her parents had burst into our hotel room (well, burst in through the open slider because while our rooms were adjoining, they were close and beachfront and…we hadn't bothered with the lock—or hell, maybe Lil had purposely left it open).

She had promised me a balloon bouquet.

And the night before, both of us naked after some serious post-getting-engaged celebration, the covers tucked up around us, me soaking in Lily's incandescent joy and knowing that her love—and her kicking my ass so that I accepted it—was the greatest gift she'd ever given me, her parents had burst in through that slider, balloons in hand.

Polaroid snapping.

I had that picture held gently in my hand as I watched the sunrise, feeling more at peace in my world than I'd ever felt before.

Living big and bright.

Another gift from Lily.

A life filled with love.

All Lily.

My ring on her finger, my love cherished in her heart.

Arms wrapping around me from behind, plucking the picture out of my hand, and I heard the smile in her voice.

"This is better than my first-time Polaroid."

I grinned, pressed a kiss to her arm. "Better fucking be."

Her legs slid around on either side of my waist, her soft scent filled my nose, the quiet crash of the waves was all around us.

Peace.

Lily.

And then she gave me even more of her.

A package in my lap.

"It's not a ring," she said lightly.

"I know," I said, light back.

"How?" A nip to my ear. "*How* do you know?"

"Maybe because this box is the size of a twelve-pack?"

She shifted, dropping into the sand in front of me. "That's because it *is* a twelve-pack," she said. "One I schlepped all the way from the States, I'll have you know. I had to leave three bikinis at home in order to make this fit."

I scowled, wondering about those bikinis and how good she'd look in them.

Then I shrugged, thinking I'd get them on her at some point so I would be able to appreciate all that *good* sooner or later.

She nudged the box.

I took the hint, tearing open the paper and wondering what kind of twelve-pack it was. I liked beer, but I didn't think I liked it well enough to schlep it from home.

Then I got a glimpse of the twelve-pack.

Not beer.

Not even close.

"Ketchup," she whispered.

My eyes prickled as I took in a box loaded with Heinz. "Fuck, I love you."

A grin. "I know." And then she rose on her knees, leaned in over that unwieldy box, and kissed me.

Tender...and then *not* tender.

Very *not* tender...until my ass became very *tender* from the freaking sand that decided to rub itself into my skin and the sun rose high enough that I didn't want to be ripe for another Polaroid campaign from her parents.

Then so *not* tender that I didn't care that I had sand in places —*all* the places.

Because then Lily took my hand and led me back to our room, and just like every time before, she took care of all the tender places.

Only this time she did it after scooping up my twelve-pack of ketchup and making sure it was safely stowed away.

Because one could never be too careful.

Because one perk of sand being in all those tender places was that it gave a girl the perfect excuse for a long-ass shower.

And, turned out, it gave Lil's parents the perfect opportunity for another Polaroid ambush.

Best. Vacation. Ever.

Want a free bonus story? Hate missing Elise's new releases? Love contests, exclusive excerpts and giveaways?
Then signup for Elise's newsletter here!
https://www.elisefaber.com/newsletter

And join Elise's fan group, the Fabinators https://www.facebook.com/groups/fabinators for insider information, sneak peaks at new releases, and fun freebies! Hope to see you there!

KTS SERIES

ALSO BY ELISE FABER

Centered

Charging

Caged

Crashed

A Gold Christmas

Cycled

Caught (February 1,2022)

Breakers Hockey (all stand alone)

Broken

Boldly

Breathless

Ballsy (April 26,2022)

Love, Action, Camera (all stand alone)

Dotted Line

Action Shot

Close-Up

End Scene

Meet Cute

Love After Midnight **(all stand alone)**

Rum And Notes

Virgin Daiquiri

On The Rocks

Sex On The Seats

Life Sucks Series **(all stand alone)**

Train Wreck

Hot Mess

Dumpster Fire

Clusterf*@k

FUBAR (March 29,2022)

Roosevelt Ranch Series **(all stand alone, series complete)**

Disaster at Roosevelt Ranch

Heartbreak at Roosevelt Ranch

Collision at Roosevelt Ranch

Regret at Roosevelt Ranch

Desire at Roosevelt Ranch

Phoenix Series **(read in order)**

Phoenix Rising

Dark Phoenix

Phoenix Freed

Phoenix: LexTal Chronicles **(rereleasing soon, stand alone, Phoenix world)**

From Ashes

In Flames

To Smoke

KTS Series

Riding The Edge

Crossing The Line

Leveling The Field

Scorching The Earth (January 25,2022)

Cocky Heroes World

Tattooed Troublemaker

ABOUT THE AUTHOR

USA Today bestselling author, Elise Faber, loves chocolate, Star Wars, Harry Potter, and hockey (the order depending on the day and how well her team -- the Sharks! -- are playing). She and her husband also play as much hockey as they can squeeze into their schedules, so much so that their typical date night is spent on the ice. Elise changes her hair color more often than some people change their socks, loves sparkly things, and is the mom to two exuberant boys. She lives in Northern California. Connect with her in her Facebook group, the Fabinators or find more information about her books at www.elisefaber.com.

f facebook.com/elisefaberauthor

a amazon.com/author/elisefaber

BB bookbub.com/profile/elise-faber

⊙ instagram.com/elisefaber

g goodreads.com/elisefaber

⑳ pinterest.com/elisefaberwrite

www.ingramcontent.com/pod-product-compliance
Lightning Source LLC
Chambersburg PA
CBHW052006240626
47153CB00008B/2761